"Cal thinks you're up to no darn good."

"And you, Sue? What do you *really* think?" For the first time Nick's voice softened.

There was no evading that piercing glance. Sue stared back at him, her eyes full of undeclared love.

"What difference does it make?" She tried to laugh. "Besides . . ."

She broke off in mid-sentence as he groaned and yanked her against him hard . . . then firm lips were parting hers. There was determination in that kiss—and a great deal more.

Other SIGNET Romance Titles by Glenna Finley You Will Enjoy

☐ **TREASURE OF THE HEART.** For the thousands of readers who have loved Emilie Loring's novels, here is the third tale of love and danger by a new novelist who blends suspense and romance with the same delightful finesse. (#T4662—75¢)

☐ **JOURNEY TO LOVE.** Beautiful Megan McLeod never thought her honeymoon would prove to be the most fateful trip of her life as she boarded a luxury liner headed for the Far East.
(#T4324—75¢)

☐ **LOVE'S HIDDEN FIRE.** A seemingly innocent work assignment and dangerous dope-smuggling ring turn into a happy ending for Diana Burke, a stylish, young interior decorator. (#T4494—75¢)

THE NEW AMERICAN LIBRARY, INC.,
P.O. Box 999, Bergenfield, New Jersey 07621

Please send me the SIGNET BOOKS I have checked above. I am enclosing $_____(check or money order—no currency or C.O.D.'s). Please include the list price plus 15¢ a copy to cover mailing costs.

Name_____

Address_____

City_____State_____Zip Code_____
Allow at least 3 weeks for delivery

Love Lies North

by
Glenna Finley

A SIGNET BOOK from
NEW AMERICAN LIBRARY
TIMES MIRROR

Copyright © 1972 by Glenna Finley

All rights reserved

SIGNET TRADEMARK REG. U.S. PAT. OFF. AND FOREIGN COUNTRIES
REGISTERED TRADEMARK—MARCA REGISTRADA
HECHO EN CHICAGO, U.S.A.

SIGNET, SIGNET CLASSICS, SIGNETTE, MENTOR AND PLUME BOOKS
*are published by The New American Library, Inc.,
1301 Avenue of the Americas, New York, New York 10019*

FIRST PRINTING, JANUARY, 1972

PRINTED IN THE UNITED STATES OF AMERICA

Brief is life but love is long,
And brief the sun of summer in the North.

—Tennyson

Chapter One

Sue Strathern stood on the rocky promontory of Wickitak Lodge and watched the stubby bow of the mail boat materialize through the pockets of early September morning mist.

The vessel, which was built in Scotland and sailed round to southeast Alaska, was about the age of the Loch Ness monster and equally as handsome. To the scattered residents on her ports of call, however, her thrice-weekly arrival was as welcome as a visit from Santa Claus. Her sturdy hull was a combination post office, freight-delivery service, and local taxicab. In addition, the latest news and gossip were delivered over her railing as cheerfully and efficiently as drums of gasoline.

This morning, the arrival was of particular interest to the young woman waiting anxiously by the steep path. She lingered at her vantage spot to wave at Captain Fergus' rotund figure in the wheelhouse and then hurried down the gravel track to the landing pier ... taking care to keep her fingers crossed en route.

"I hope to heaven he found someone to get me out of trouble," she muttered fervently as she made her way past dripping undergrowth.

She pulled up sharply when an overhanging hemlock branch pulled her chiffon headscarf onto her shoulders. For a moment, the pale fall sunshine gleamed on her coppery hair before she hurriedly replaced the scarf and moved on down to the pier as the boat nudged up to the dock.

A tall man, standing by Captain Fergus, let out a soft whistle as he noted her trim figure, set off by slim slacks and hip-hugging nylon jacket.

"I told you she was pretty, Mr. Dunbar." The captain still rolled his r's as if he'd left Glasgow the week before rather than thirty years ago. "It's a good thing that Wickitak is isolated or the men in this part of the country would be standing in line at the gate. Imagine finding a beautiful copper-nob who has some sense, as well!" He spun the wheel casually as he kept a sharp eye on the dock. "Coming up here on her vacations to stay with an uncle probably helped her keep the right perspective on things. Tim's on a holiday himself right now—that's why Sue is playing landlady in his place." He glanced over at the intent figure by his side. "Ever since that Indian couple of Tim's took off for Juneau, she's been on her own up here ... although Cal Martin and his Northland Flying Service are at her beck and call if she needs anything."

"Why? Is he a special friend or does she own

stock in the company?" There was only casual curiosity in Nicholas Dunbar's deep voice.

Fergus chuckled. "Cal would like to hand her fifty percent of the stock on a platter."

"What's holding things up?"

"He wants a marriage certificate in return. The talk around these parts is that Sue is asking for more time to make up her mind. Damn these pockets of fog!" He ducked his head out the door and shouted to his crewman at the bow. "Get ready to heave that line, Jim! Miss Strathern'll make it fast." He turned back to his passenger. "Sorry to have to unload you in such a hurry this morning but I'm way behind schedule."

"That's all right." The other man zipped up the front of his jacket and reached down for the big suitcase stowed nearby. "I appreciate the lift."

"No trouble. That's what I'm here for." Fergus was intent on holding his ship steady in the strong current caused by the junction of a swift-flowing river and the saltwater channel. "Jim will toss your bag up after you get on the pier."

"Right. Thanks again, Captain."

The older man sketched a brief salute and watched his passenger stride easily down the slippery deck and hand the suitcase to Jim. Then Dunbar took a few seconds to gauge the rolling motion of the boat and jumped easily onto the pier. Sue was standing nearby, ready to loosen the forward line.

"Sling up the bag, Jim," Fergus bellowed from the wheelhouse. "Sorry I can't stop to shoot the breeze wi' ya, Sue. I'll be bringin' out your order on the next trip and have more time then."

Sue, whose eyes had widened at the impact of the stranger on the dock beside her, heard Fergus' words but didn't entirely comprehend them. "What about the mail, Captain?" she called.

"I gave it to Mr. Dunbar." He gestured toward the man who was now watching the proceedings after catching his bag and putting it back by the path. "Cast off now, lass . . ." The rest of his sentence was drowned in the increased revs of the engine, and Sue smiled with resignation before she reached down to loosen the line on the bollard.

"Let me. . . ." Dunbar was matter-of-fact as he moved in to release the heavy manila hawser and cast it back on the deck as the mail boat backed away.

"I can do it," Sue protested and then clutched frantically at his sleeve as the landing stage surged crazily in the wake of the heavy craft.

"I'm sure you can," Nick told her amusedly as he watched her regain her balance and then drop his sleeve as if it were red-hot. "What about continuing this discussion on solid land before we fall into the drink?"

Still confused at the swift interchange, Sue summoned enough presence of mind to wave farewell to Captain Fergus before she led the way off the dock.

Once on the beginning of the path, she stopped abruptly and turned to face the man following in her footsteps. "I'm Sue Strathern," she said firmly, as if determined to get their relationship on a solid footing, as well. "I'm certainly glad you turned up in answer to my ad. Frankly, I didn't have much hope of getting anyone at such short notice. Did Captain Fergus give you any clues about the job here at the lodge?"

"Not exactly...."

She nodded briskly. "That's all right. You look strong enough to handle all the chores, Mr.... I'm sorry," she made an apologetic gesture with her hands—"I wasn't functioning when Captain Fergus mentioned your name."

"It's Dunbar," he said. "Nick Dunbar."

"Mr. Dunbar," she repeated. "Have you ever done a caretaker's job before? To be honest, you aren't quite the type I had in mind."

Her eyes ran a yardstick over the man in front of her and left her with a puzzled expression. He was tall but of a wiry build rather than sheer muscular bulk and was in his early thirties. Straight dark brown hair was slicked neatly back from a high forehead, and he met her glance with one of his own from piercing gray eyes. His tanned skin stretched tightly over a slightly aquiline nose and a lean, strong jaw. If he was suffering any uneasiness from her perusal, it wasn't apparent. A bulky nylon jacket topped khaki trousers, which, in turn, were tucked into rugged hiking boots—the standard outfit for Alaskan bush country.

Her glance flicked upward again to meet that quizzical, direct gaze. "I was thinking of an older man," she murmured. "Do you have any references?"

"Not with me, but don't let appearances put you off. They can be deceiving on both sides." His voice was easy. "I didn't expect to come across an employer like you."

This time it was his masculine gaze doing the surveying ... starting at the vibrant coppery hair, wandering down past indignant deep blue eyes, lingering over the creamy skin of a pert nose to finally arrive at rounded lips, which, at the moment, were thinned to a forbidding line.

"You'll recognize me again," she told him coolly. "Appearances might be deceiving but as you don't have any written references"—her voice was edged with sarcasm—"possibly you might tell me something about your background?"

"Sure thing. What did you have in mind?" Amusement lurked under his words.

"For one thing—how does it happen that you're in this part of the country?"

"I was visiting friends in Juneau. . . ." he started cautiously.

"And you saw my ad in the paper?"

"You could say that."

"You do understand that this is just a temporary job," she pursued. "My uncle's regular caretaker cut his leg when he was clearing brush and has another week or two in the hospital. His wife will be back in the next day or so, though, to take over the cooking."

He was searching in his jacket pocket for a pack of cigarettes. "The cooking shouldn't be much of a problem for just the two of us."

"There'll be more than two, Mr. Dunbar." She shook her head as he offered the opened pack. "I'm expecting three other people to be staying at the lodge from tomorrow on."

"Oh?" He used his lighter on a cigarette with an economy of motion. "I thought the season was over."

"Officially, it is. Evidently these people made special reservations with my uncle before he left on his vacation. That's why I need help. With Joe Laperouse out of action, I need a man to take care of the boats, replenish our wood supply, and to service the motor generator for our electricity. Did you have any experience along those lines?" She paused and her voice took on an edge: "While you were visiting your friends in Juneau."

He ignored the jibe. "I've messed about with boats, but I'm certainly not any Alaskan fishing guide."

"Don't worry about that," she told him carelessly. "The cohos are running, so if you can just get the cruiser out into midchannel without ramming an iceberg, they should be able to get their limit." She gestured toward his bag. "If you want to bring that along, we can talk on our way back to the lodge."

He reached down for it and then fell into step beside her. "This looks like quite a place. Does your uncle's property take up the whole peninsula?"

She nodded. "Plus some adjoining mainland. He homesteaded it years ago. This was an offshore island until he brought in some fill for a causeway. The steep rock sides of the property make it almost like a fortress and Uncle Tim put in a high iron gate on the causeway road. It has to be a pretty determined bear or wolf that can get out here." She brushed aside a soaked spruce branch as they climbed back up the winding trail. "That satisfied all of Uncle Tim's customers. Supposedly, they come up here to rough it at a hunting lodge and visit the glaciers, but they aren't keen about colliding with a black bear before breakfast." She chuckled suddenly. "Although Uncle Tim said that usually the bears were more appalled than the visitors."

"I can imagine."

"Anyhow, now he has the causeway gate and everything's serene." She hesitated. "Would you like to rest? This is a pretty steep climb unless you're used to it."

He caught the glint of a challenge in her look. "Thanks, but I can manage." He glanced ahead and gave a low whistle as he glimpsed a long, rambling structure. "So that's Wickitak Lodge."

"Uncle Tim's pride and joy."

"Small wonder." He moved on slowly, letting his gaze cover the steep-gabled, two-storied building. Weathered cedar roof shakes blended into silvery timbers which looked sturdy enough to outlast the most violent Alaskan gale. A massive native stone fireplace occupied one wall of the lounge at the front and long thermopane windows provided a frame for the magnificent view down onto the channel and the river. Deep, overhanging eaves protected a wide porch along one side of the structure.

Squarely at the end of the path, by the porch steps, stood a huge black and tan animal that greeted Nick with a fierce, rumbling growl.

Nick pulled up abruptly. "Good lord, what's that?"

"What do you think?" Sue countered defensively. "It's a dog of course . . . Uncle Tim's dog. Possibly he's slightly oversized. . . ."

"Oversized! My God, he looks big enough to eat hay." Nick continued to stare. "What's that in his mouth?"

"Just a stick. I imagine he stole it from the hearth." She leaned over and petted the massive head. "It's all right, Rock—this is Mr. Dunbar. Don't eat him; he's staying awhile."

The growling stopped and the crook of a tail wagged tentatively as the big dog approached Nick, who bent down and scratched gently behind an ear on the offered head.

"Rock, is it? As in . . ."

"As in marble, granite, and native stone," Sue said wryly. "Whenever he makes up his mind, he comes in the same category. He's as big and unswerving as a freight train, but in his heart he cherishes the notion that he's a lap dog." She smiled. "It's like cuddling King Kong."

"He looks like the original shaggy dog."

"He wouldn't—if he were decently trimmed," Sue told him. "Actually, under all that hair there is a perfectly civilized Airedale. Uncle Tim just lets him go bush."

"And carry around tree stumps." Nick watched as the terrier stomped solemnly up the porch steps and collapsed with a sigh by the front door.

"He shreds them like a beaver all over the

lodge," Sue admitted as they went up the steps and through the massive front door. "It's a wonder he doesn't have splinters lining his entire stomach." She watched Nick put down his suitcase by the foot of the curving stair. "The first rule at Wickitak is 'Don't Walk Around Barefoot' or you'll be crippled for life." She motioned toward the big lounge at their left. "If you'd like to go in and be comfortable, I'll find you some coffee."

"Thanks very much. Captain Fergus does make his departures at the crack of dawn. Some coffee should help to wake me up." He watched her cross the room to a coffee urn in an alcove by the bar and switch on the heat. Then his gaze wandered to take in the roughly carved beams supporting the high, vaulted ceiling of the lounge. Apparently the rustic touch stopped with the beams as a deep gold carpet covered the slate flooring and oversized black leather davenports flanked the huge stone fireplace wall. Under the wide windows, occasional chairs in shades of citron and sunshine yellow brought warmth into the room and blended easily with the green vegetation beyond the glass.

He walked over to the window and stared out at the magnificent view. The mountains looked as if they had been provided in multicolored layers; there was dark foliage in the foothills but occasionally the ribbon trail of an old avalanche would be bright green, looking like an appliquéd patch on the darker color of the hillside.

The higher shapes in the distance were still diffused by the gray, misty haze which hid their flaws as a diffusion lens would hide wrinkles on an aging subject. At the very back there rose a monumental snowcapped peak—perhaps content to remain in the background because its beauty immediately became the focus of any admiring eyes.

"The mist is burning off quickly." Sue had come up by his side. "That's a sign of early fall."

He nodded. "With a view like this, I'm surprised your uncle wanted to leave home."

"He doesn't very often. Actually, a friend of his made it hard to refuse. He was going on a photographic safari to east Africa and insisted that Uncle Tim join him as his guest. The chance of seeing all those elephants in Mozambique was too great a temptation." She reached up to unzip her jacket and drop it on the back of a chair. "I'll show you to your room after we've had the coffee."

"Thanks." He shrugged off his jacket as he watched her trim figure move gracefully away in the direction of the coffee urn. It flickered through his mind that not many women could look so completely feminine in a pair of whipcord slacks and a tailored green wool shirt.

Just then the shaggy Airedale came slowly into the room still carrying his firewood. He moved over to the fireplace hearth and squatted down before shifting his burden and starting to chew on it with evident enjoyment.

"Is passing through closed doors another of his talents?" Nick asked with interest.

Sue looked over her shoulder from the filling of the coffee mugs and shook her head. "He doesn't need to. There's a special pet door around by the back entrance." She put the coffee on a tray along with sugar and a cream pitcher from the small, stainless steel refrigerator by the bar. Carrying the tray back to the window, she glanced over to see the log being methodically shredded into bite-sized chunks. "That's what I mean," she said resignedly.

"They could use him in a pulp mill." Nick was grinning as he moved an ashtray so that she could rest the tray on a table beside him.

"Maybe Uncle Tim could hire him out a half day at a time. It might offset the bill for dog food. Speaking of food..." she glanced up at him, "would you like a sweet roll to go with this? Things are a little thin in the kitchen since the cook's been gone, but I can manage that."

"No thanks... this coffee will do fine." He took an appreciative sip. "It must have been lonesome for you here on your own."

"A little," she acknowledged, "although it's

not as bad as it might seem. I check in with our flying service by radio each morning and evening. In case of an emergency, Cal Martin would be here inside of an hour. That's how we got Joe to the hospital so quickly when he hurt his leg." She added sugar to her coffee and stirred it. "Captain Fergus stops by with the mail boat three times a week, and there's quite a bit of fishing traffic in the main channel. I suppose I could get a distress signal to them if I couldn't manage any other way."

"Just like Times Square."

"In some ways. On the other hand, I haven't been strolling by the glacier on the trimline trails since I've been by myself. Uncle Tim left specific instructions about that. While we're near the lodge, this is safe territory. Once you start wandering on the mainland, it pays to know what you're doing. Even the cheechako knows that."

"And you're not exactly a Cheechako newcomer, are you?"

She raised her coffee mug in response to his translation. "Actually, I am. Did those friends of yours in Juneau clue you in on the slang around here?"

"Enough to get by." He watched her settle into an overstuffed chair and sat down on the one next to it. "So you're not native to these parts?"

She shook her head. "Just a visitor. When I

was in college, there wasn't enough time for extended vacations and for the last two years, I've been working in New York."

"That's a far cry from running a hunting lodge."

"Not as far as you might think," she said ruefully. "You see before you a grossly underpaid writer for trade magazines. We print monthly publications like the *Sheet-Metal Gazette* and the *Floor-Covering Digest*. The articles are so dull that even the subscribers don't bother to read them." She took another sip of coffee and surveyed the toes of her shoes. "During the past two years, I've been assigned to most of them. Lately, one of the editors heard that I had an uncle living in Alaska and he immediately put me on *Outdoor Man* . . . a publication for distributors of camping and hunting equipment." She looked up at his sudden chuckle. "It's not funny . . . they're expecting me to come back chockful of ideas about hunting and trapping."

"And you don't intend to cooperate?"

"I couldn't snare a rabbit . . . much less hurt anything as beautiful as a Dall sheep. And if these guests of Uncle Tim expect great things in the hunting line, they're going to be disappointed too." Her gaze flickered over him. "Unless you're a great outdoorsman?"

"Sorry . . . I don't qualify. If they want to be ridden around on a boat, I can manage to keep them on board. That's all. I'm not even up on the latest lures and lines for this part of the country."

She waved an impatient hand. "Don't worry about that. Uncle Tim has all kinds of fishing gear in the boathouse."

"Where's that?"

"On the opposite side from the dock where the mail boat came in." She stood up and went to the window. "You can see the roof of it from here." She felt his tall figure move over beside her. "The lean-to beside it houses our jeep...." Suddenly she felt her breathing quicken as if she'd been running hard and she deliberately went back to her chair, leaving him to stand alone by the glass. "Only don't count on the jeep because it's out of commission at the moment."

He looked back at her over his shoulder. "Oh? So we're confined to water transportation, eh?"

If she noticed the collective pronoun, she didn't mention it. "One power cruiser and a glorified rowboat with an outboard. Any other movement is strictly shank's mare."

He strolled over to survey a framed map by the fireplace. "I notice your uncle has the trails marked on this—there's quite a bit of property."

"Over six hundred acres. Years ago, Uncle Tim took me around the boundaries, but I couldn't find them all now." She put her coffee mug down on a table and went over beside him. "You can see that Wickitak property abuts the national forest." Her slim finger traced the black lines on the map. "My uncle just has a sliver of land up in here—there's the glacier to the north and the national forest extending all the way down south. As you get nearer the water, it spreads more into the pie shape you can see there." She flicked at the map dispassionately. "Don't worry about the boundaries too much. The trails are pretty well marked but since we're not familiar with the terrain, I'll warn the guests not to stray far. Up here, the expanses are too great." She went back to retrieve her coffee and perch on the arm of her chair. "Besides, I don't think this threesome will wander."

Nick gave the map a final glance and then moved back beside her. "Who are they?"

"There's a retired schoolteacher named Florence Davis..." She broke off in midsentence to watch Rock abruptly abandon his mounting pile of chips and stalk over behind the bar. He reemerged with a dog biscuit which he proceeded to demolish by her feet. "You'll notice that Rock is very fond of eating out," she said ruefully as she scratched his back with her shoe. "He eats out in the dining room, out in the bedroom annex, and out here in the lounge. Practically everywhere except out of his bowl in the kitchen."

"A psychiatrist could have a field day with him," Nick said gravely as he reached down to offer a crumb the long nose had overlooked. It was sniffed at and then consumed methodically. "Who else is there besides Miss Davis?"

"Miss Davis?" Sue's thoughts had wandered. "Oh ... *that* Miss Davis. Let's see, there's her nephew Leo and a secretary. She didn't give a clue to the secretary's sex or identity."

"Where are they from?"

"Their letter was airmailed from Chicago."

He fumbled in his shirt pocket and offered his cigarettes.

"No thanks, I don't smoke," she said, pushing a glass ashtray nearer for his convenience.

He nodded his thanks and used a pack of matches from the table. "How long are they staying?"

"They've booked for ten days." Her brows drew together in a sudden frown. "I can't understand how Uncle Tim happened to accept their reservation in the first place. He canceled all the others when he knew he was going to be away. Of course, he had no way of knowing that Joe was going to get hurt and that Marie would go down to Juneau while he was in the hospital." She gave him a level glance. "Quite frankly, I'm delighted you applied for the job. I could probably have managed to muddle through but Wickitak's reputation would certainly have suffered."

"We'll manage." Nick drew deeply on his cigarette and then snubbed it out before standing up. "I'd better get to work." He grinned as the big Airedale got to his feet and looked up attentively. "Am I going to have an overseer?"

"You'll undoubtedly have company," she promised. "Rock's tired of following me around. Just make sure he stays behind the gate."

"How is he on the trail?"

"Very good ... but he isn't allowed to roam on the mainland." She reached down and patted the rough head affectionately. "One thing about Airedales ... they have terrific stamina. That's necessary in this country."

He nodded. "I imagine so. Shall I take my bag up to my room?"

"Of course." She led the way through the dining area toward the main stair. "The kitchen's at the back. ... Joe and Marie have their quarters just beyond. The bedrooms are on the second story." She started up the carpeted treads, which curved around a huge peeled tree trunk reaching to roof level.

Nick admired it as they wound upward. "This was a real giant."

"Too nice to take away. Uncle Tim insisted they leave it when the lodge was enlarged a few years ago." She opened a door at the head of the stairs. "You should be comfortable in here. The bath adjoins and has a second door on the hall." She nodded toward the end of the corridor. "I'll put the Davis party down in the three-room suite. I've taken over Uncle Tim's bedroom and study across from you. With all of us on the same corridor, it will simplify the heating."

"My quarters look fine." He was glancing over the comfortable room decorated in cheerful tones of gold and brown. His lips twitched as he turned back to her. "I didn't expect anything this luxurious with the job."

"We aim to please," she assured him and devoutly hoped he wouldn't notice the bunk room by the back door which had been readied for the temporary caretaker.

"Where's the pooch?"

"Probably down on the porch waiting for you. You won't be able to call your soul your own from now on.... Big Brother doesn't watch over you at Wickitak but Rocko does." Her grin was mischievous. "Those brown eyes of his will be fixed on everything you do. He's not smart but he *is* persistent."

"In that case, he and I can pool our ignorance." His slow smile matched hers. "Thanks for the job, Miss Strathern. I'll see you later on."

Sue was halfway to the kitchen before she realized that she still knew next to nothing about her new caretaker. She had systematically told him about Uncle Tim, the lodge, and their expected guests. In between, she had sandwiched Rock's history and her own.

As an interviewer he had been superb.

The only tidbit she had gleaned was that Nicholas Dunbar was undoubtedly the most attractive man she had ever met in her life.

Chapter Two

"So this is where you've gotten to!" Nick said the next morning as he pushed through the side door onto the barbecue patio and found Sue standing in front of a feebly smoking fireplace.

"Was I lost?" Pushing back her jacket cuff, she looked at her watch. "Oh lord, it's almost eight o'clock. . . . I suppose you want some breakfast." She surveyed his waiting form nervously, unconsciously noting the casual khaki trousers and plaid shirt with sleeves rolled up to reveal muscular forearms as tanned as his face. His hair was neatly combed and still damp from the shower.

A billow of smoke in front of her face caused her to look hastily back at the smoldering fire and then at the pan on the grill above it. The yellow gelatinous mess still remained stubbornly in its original form.

"Damn!" she said explosively and turned defiantly back to Nick. "Are you very hungry?"

Her onslaught didn't appear to daunt him. "Don't panic," he said calmly as he moved over to sit on the bench of a wooden picnic table. "I wasn't sure what time I was supposed to make an appearance but Rock insisted on seven-thirty."

She clapped a hand to the side of her head. "Omigosh—I meant to warn you that you'd be blessed with his presence in the morning unless the hall door's tightly latched. I hoped you didn't mind."

"Nope . . . I'm getting conditioned to his ways. It was a little unnerving to find him eating dog biscuits over the bathtub last night but I fished most of his crumbs out of the water." He grinned at her embarrassed features. "They probably had as much therapeutic effect as the Epsom salts I'd dumped in. At least, I'm not quite so stiff this morning."

"It's no wonder you were stiff ... you shouldn't have used that chain saw as long as you did. There must be enough firewood cut to last for weeks. Joe will certainly be delighted when he comes back."

"I'll try to have a backlog for him. After a siege in the hospital, he won't be in condition for that kind of work." He stirred restlessly on the bench. "What's on the agenda for today?"

She gave the contents of the frying pan another desperate stir. "After breakfast, you mean. I was going to have this ready, but now it looks as if it needs another hour."

"Unless you get that grill closer to the fire, I think two hours would be more accurate." He stood up and approached her warily. "Mind a little help?"

"My pride is fractured," she admitted, stepping back to get out of the smoke, "but frankly, I'm starving too. Be my guest."

He quickly sized up the situation and disposed of the frying pan on the wooden picnic table. Then taking a kitchen towel from a nearby tray, he folded it for use as a hot pad and moved the grill down to its lowest position over the smoldering fire. The next step was to cut shavings from small pieces of firewood stacked nearby and pile them on the coals. Within minutes, he had coaxed the blaze to burn briskly. As if mesmerized, Sue watched him go over to retrieve the frying pan and stare down at its contents before replacing it on the grill.

He shot her a quizzical glance. "Okay . . . I give up. What is it?"

"Would you believe I put too much water in the dehydrated eggs?"

He ran the spoon through the liquid and shuddered visibly. "I'll take your word for it."

She came to peer over his shoulder. "Can it be salvaged?"

"You want my frank opinion?" he asked.

Her lips twitched with amusement. "Spare me and scratch one experiment. Actually, I was doing some homework for my job."

He looked up from disposing of the remains.

"What connection is there between dehydrated eggs and writing articles for a camping magazine? Don't tell me that ..." his voice trailed off and the fine laughter lines beside his eyes deepened" ... you're the Julia Child of the wilderness?"

"Not yet, but I've been appointed food editor for the thing," she confessed. "It's about as appropriate as appointing Rip Van Winkle to sound reveille. I can have trouble deciding whether to use white or yellow corn meal in a tamale pie."

"I didn't notice any disasters over dinner last night."

She shoved her hands in the pockets of her slacks. "It isn't very difficult to mix a salad and put a steak under the broiler at the crucial time. But as for Hunters' Breakfasts ..." her shoulders drooped, "either I'll inadvertently poison our entire subscription list or get fired trying." She flopped down on the picnic bench. "Yesterday, after forty-five minutes, I managed to burn canned bacon over a campfire. The day before, I put too much water in my pancake batter and tried to thicken it with some instant oatmeal. You should have seen the results! I fed one pancake to Rock and he sulked for hours afterwards." She made a sweeping gesture. "You'll notice he isn't around—even now. I tell you that dog's smarter than you think."

Nick chuckled. "In another five minutes, I'm

apt to be in munching on his dog biscuits if something isn't done. I gather that it isn't necessary for us to eat dried eggs?"

"Heavens no!" The words were a sigh of defeat as she got up and took the tray from his hands. "There's a refrigerator full of the real thing. We might as well go into the kitchen and I'll cook breakfast there." She put her head to one side and gave him a mocking look. "I *can* manage that."

"I'm sure you could but why not have it out here now that the fire's going. It's a shame to waste this sunshine."

"But I told you . . . I ruin everything on that grill."

"Then you can watch me," he assured her. "It's not *cordon bleu*, but we'll eat. One summer when I was in college, I signed on as camp cook for a dude ranch that featured trail breakfasts. Fortunately, I was a fast learner and everybody survived my efforts." He leveled the coals in the fire. "Now—lead me to that refrigerator."

Forty-five minutes later, Sue was swallowing the last bite of a jam-covered biscuit. "I didn't think it was possible," she said, pausing to lick her finger before reaching over to the tray for another paper napkin.

"Think what was possible?" Nick took his coffee mug and moved off the hard bench onto a reclining chair.

"That anything so good to eat could come from over a campfire." She scrubbed her lips and, picking up her coffee mug, followed him to an adjoining chair. "The most devastating blow though, was when Rock looked out and decided to stay on." She nodded to a spot under the table where the big dog had happily collapsed after sampling all offerings.

"Strictly cupboard love."

"Ummm ... but humiliating all the same." She took a swallow of coffee. "Did I warn you that I intend to filch all your ideas and double our magazine's circulation?"

"Just keep the bicarbonate of soda handy." He leaned back lazily. "What time do you expect your customers?"

She looked at her watch. "Any minute now. When I talked to Cal this morning, he said the flight from the south was a little late. There was bad weather when they tried to land at Annette Island."

"Martin sounds like a handy fellow to have at the other end of a radio."

"He is," she said enthusiastically. "Financing a small flying service is difficult for a man in his mid-twenties, but Cal is finally getting his equipment paid for."

The slight breeze stirred a napkin on the table and they both watched its brief flight.

Sue took a deep breath. "I love September

up here. The clear days are as crisp and tangy as a Jonathan apple."

"Then you'd better cherish the memory of this sunshine because it's about to disappear. Take a look at those clouds."

She stared obediently upward. During breakfast, the sky had lost all its pastel colors and clouded over in shades of silver and gray. To the north and west, forbidding black billows were gathering on the horizon.

"I didn't know there had been such a change. Your breakfast was so good that it took my mind off practical things." She glanced at her watch again before getting up and starting to pile their dishes on a tray. "Cal might have to hurry if he's going to deposit our passengers on schedule. He'll probably have to take a rain check on lunch too."

Nick stood up. "I'd better go down and look over the cruiser in case your customers want to go out fishing this afternoon."

"It might not be a bad idea. Uncle Tim keeps all the things like marine charts and copies of the *Alaska Sport Fishing Guide* on the desk in his study."

"I'll take a look at them," he promised.

"Why don't you go on up now? These dishes won't take a minute and I don't need any help in the kitchen."

"Let me carry that coffeepot, at least." He followed her up the porch steps and held the door open for her. "Did you say your uncle's study adjoined his bedroom?"

She nodded. "That's right ... just walk on through. My occupancy hasn't made much of a dent in the masculine surroundings. I've kept all his notes together on his desk rather than spreading them around the lounge...." She paused in midsentence as the drone of an airplane engine suddenly penetrated the atmosphere. "That's Cal now! I'd better get these dishes out of the way."

He trailed in her wake into the big stainless-steel-equipped kitchen and put the coffeepot on the back burner of the stove. "There's still enough in there to revive the guests if they want some."

"Good!" She deposited the tray of dishes on an immaculate counter-top. "These can wait. Let's get down to the float and see if Cal needs any help."

"Better put this on ... that wind's getting chilly." He plucked her jacket off an oak hall tree and held it for her before shrugging into his as they went out on the porch. By then, the sound of the plane engine was much louder. "Where does he put down?"

"Usually by the boathouse. We've a special ramp there and the current isn't as strong as it is where the mail boat ties up."

She was leading him down a curving path behind the lodge which was twin to the one they had climbed the day before. The whine of the engine was like the buzzing of an angry bee as it filtered through the trees.

"By golly, I think he brought the bigger Cessna," her words tumbled together in the excitement.

"Is that good?"

"I should say so! We'll know in a minute... just as soon as we get around this bend." She pulled up to look as the path suddenly dropped down onto the gravel track leading to the boathouse.

A silver and red floatplane was taxiing up the side of the broad glacial river making for the landing ramp at the end of the building. A narrow catwalk made of tubular metal led from the sheltered area under the eaves of the boathouse down to the water.

Sue turned an animated face up to Nick. "That's the Cessna 206, so that means Cal has brought Marie along. He evidently convinced her that we needed her more than Joe does right now."

"How do you know all this?"

"Because this plane carries five passengers." She raised her voice to carry over the sound of the engine as they moved quickly along the side of the boathouse. "If he'd just brought three people, he'd have used a smaller plane. Watch your step on this catwalk... it's a little tricky."

He nodded and then there was no more conversation while they watched the floatplane being brought neatly into the quiet water in front of them. As the pilot cut his engine, Sue moved a protective metal guard on the post at the end of the walk and pushed a button. There was the hum of an engine motor in the boathouse behind them and a square platform of the metal tubing came slowly up under the plane to support the pontoons securely. Water drained out through the mesh at the edges.

Within half a minute, the pilot had the plane door opened and was jumping out to pull Sue into a bear hug. "How's my best girl?" he asked happily as he finally put her back to arm's length and stood beaming down at her. "Just as beautiful as ever, I see."

"Stop it, Cal!" She shrugged out of his embrace easily. "Are you going to leave your passengers incarcerated in there? You'd better give them a hand."

"All right . . . but don't go away." He bounded back to the open door of the plane where a gray-haired woman wearing a tweed suit was looking down at the platform with some trepidation. "Let me help you, Miss Davis."

Shaking her head in amusement, Sue glanced over at Nick who was quietly watching the scene. "I'll introduce you in a minute. Cal's such a crazy galoot . . . he finds all sorts of distractions."

"So I noticed," he said in a level voice as he watched the tall, sandy-haired pilot cheerfully disgorge his passengers. He handled them easily, his powerful shoulder muscles evident under a close-fitting gray uniform shirt bearing the insignia of the Northland Flying Service. His overall appearance was on the rugged side with a nose that looked as if it had been broken and reset casually some years before, but the directness of his intelligent gaze could not be discounted. A strong chin and jaw line belied the easy amiability he was displaying to the people around him. All things considered, he looked like a young man who could be pushed only in the direction he had previously planned to follow. Nick turned his attention to the others; the gray-haired lady was clutching an oversized tote bag and smiling at a middle-aged Indian woman who was stepping onto the platform with an easy familiarity. She carried a small overnight case and briskly nodded her thanks to Cal before making her way toward them.

"Marie! You're as welcome as the flowers of May. I hope it was all right with Joe that you came back to help us out." Sue caught her around the waist and pulled her over toward Nick. "This is Mr. Dunbar . . . he's helping out until Joe can come back. Mr. Dunbar—Marie Laperouse."

"I'm happy to know you, Marie." Nick shook

hands. "Miss Strathern has told me what a fine job you and your husband do at the lodge."

The other's dark eyes flashed appreciatively. "Thank you, Mr. Dunbar. It will be nice to be back in my own kitchen again after staying with relatives down in Juneau."

"How is Joe?" Sue asked.

"Just fine," his wife told her, beaming. "He's in good enough condition to be flirting with his nurses so he can do without me for a while. Mr. Cal says he'll fly me down to check on him one of these afternoons." She pulled her coat closer around her stout waist. "Now I'll get on up to the lodge and get settled in. I'll check with you, Miss Sue, after I've looked at the stores."

"Fine, Marie."

They watched her stride up the walk and then turned back to greet the trio Cal was escorting toward them. The pleasant, gray-haired woman was in front and still clutching her tote bag as if it contained precious cargo.

Sue extended a welcoming hand. "It's Miss Davis, isn't it? I'm Sue Strathern."

"Florence Davis," the other confirmed in a well-modulated voice, "and I'm so glad to be here."

"We were glad you made it before there was a break in the weather," Sue said. "May I present Nicholas Dunbar who's helping me in my uncle's absence." She colored slightly under Nick's suddenly wry expression, which told her he had noted the rapid promotion from caretaker to assistant manager.

"How do you do, Miss Davis." He was careful to keep his amusement hidden.

"And this is my nephew, Leo," Florence said fondly, pulling forward a stocky man in his early forties whose tousled black hair matched the untidy appearance of a wrinkled business suit. "He looks a little the worse for wear, but airplanes do that to people. Miss Strathern, Leo, and Mr. Dunbar."

Leo pushed his heavy, horn-rimmed glasses up a prominent nose before shaking hands apathetically. "Thank god, we're finally on the ground! My stomach's going to be upset for a week after this jaunt. Just lead me to my room."

"In a minute, Leo," his aunt said firmly. "Let me introduce Monica first." She looked briskly over her shoulder. "Come, my dear, we're all waiting for you."

"I'm sorry, Florence." The vision that had been standing close to Cal moved toward them. "I was asking Mr. Martin about some of the glacier flights." She gave Nick a ravishing smile which barely included Sue in its periphery. "I'm Monica Templeton, Mr. Davis' secretary."

"I'm Sue Strathern." If Sue's voice was flat it was mainly because she was astounded by the fashionable vision in front of her. Monica

Templeton was a ravishing brunette who could have been a successful candidate for the centerfold of *Playboy* any month of the year. Surrounded by Florence and Leo, it was as if Aphrodite had skipped down from heaven to spend a long weekend with a couple of the lower mortals. She was elegantly attired in a plum-colored pants suit whose expensive lines outlined her tall and voluptuous figure. In flat heels, she could look her employer squarely in the eye, but at the moment, her eyes were busily inspecting Wickitak's new assistant manager. "May I present Mr. Dunbar," Sue said dryly.

"I'm happy to know you, Miss Templeton," he acknowledged. "Let me help you and Miss Davis with those bags."

He needn't, thought Sue, have been so quick off the mark with the offer.

"No thanks," Florence declined for both of them. "Monica's used to carrying her vanity case and I'd feel lost without this tote bag." She looked over to Sue. "Perhaps we could get on up to the lodge...."

"Of course," Sue sent a mental apology to Uncle Tim for her wandering thoughts and became an official hostess again. "Follow the path and you'll be up at the lodge in no time. Just make yourselves at home in the lounge, and we'll be there shortly." She watched the older woman move up the ramp followed by

Monica, who wafted an effortless smile down on Cal and Nick.

"Watch your step, Monica!" Leo nodded jerkily in their direction before he followed his secretary up the ramp. "This isn't the place to get a broken ankle."

"But she'd look nice with one, wouldn't she?" Cal countered in a low tone as he came up to Sue. "Can't you see her in a velvet housecoat draped over a davenport in the lounge? It's a good thing for you, Susie, that my taste runs to redheads instead of brunettes."

"Your taste, Mr. Martin," she said tartly, "runs through every shade on the hair chart. If you can drag your mind back to business, this is Nicholas Dunbar."

"Hi. I've heard about you." The warmth in Cal's voice faded abruptly as he shook hands with Nick. He was scowling as he turned back to Sue. "You left out a few details when you talked to me . . . maybe it was on purpose."

Her cheeks reddened under his intent gaze. "I don't know what you mean."

"Don't pull that old saw." He shoved his hands in his pockets and teetered back on his heels. "Somehow I got the impression that Mr. Dunbar here was a good twenty years older."

Nick broke in quickly and diplomatically. "After I finished cutting wood yesterday, I felt at least ninety . . . and I haven't recovered yet." He turned toward the plane. "I'd better start moving their luggage up to the lodge; Leo didn't look like the patient type."

"Be with you in a minute," Cal assured him. In a lower tone he said to Sue "Since when is a guy like that working as a caretaker?"

"Since yesterday, at least. What's wrong with that?"

"Not a thing except that he talks like a university professor, wears expensive, custom-made hiking boots, and is big enough to go hunting bear with a switch. If Dunbar's a typical caretaker, I'm a monkey's uncle."

She gave him an impatient push toward the plane. "Remember, you said it ... I didn't. You might give him a hand with the bags, anyhow."

His pleasant face twisted in exasperation. "All right, but I suspect you're trying to palm me off."

"Don't be silly—I invited you to lunch."

"Can't do it today. I still have to deliver some spare parts up the inlet to Five Mile Camp." He glanced overhead. "From the way those clouds are rolling in, it's straight back for Juneau after that."

She nodded understandingly. "I'll give you the usual rain check."

"Sooner than you think, chum. Miss Templeton ..." he grinned at her expression as he drawled the secretary's name, "can't wait to see Glacier Bay monument, so I'm to fly the whole party in the day after tomorrow for an overnight stay at the inn up there."

She smiled. "The news doesn't break my heart. As a landlady, I suspect I'll leave a lot to be desired. Thank goodness, Marie's back to feed them."

"And Dunbar's around to help entertain them. Monica will appreciate that."

"No doubt," she said coolly, refusing to rise to the bait. "I'll see you the day after tomorrow then."

"Maybe I can convince you to come down to Juneau for the weekend," he said coaxingly. "Wickitak will slog along now that Marie's back and Dunbar's on the premises."

"Taking my name in vain?" Nick appeared beside them with a bag in each hand and a camera bag slung over his shoulder.

Cal shook his head. "Just trying to set up a date with Sue for the weekend. I told her Wickitak didn't need its hand held now that you're around."

"That's right. If Miss Strathern wants to go, I think I can keep the wolves from the door. Nice to have met you, Martin. If you'll sling those other two bags up by the boathouse, I'll get them on the next trip down."

"See what I mean," Cal said helplessly as he watched Nick stride up the ramp. "I almost ended up by pulling at my forelock and saying

'Yes sir, Mr. Dunbar—thank you, sir.' If that man's a caretaker. . . ."

"I know . . . you're a monkey's uncle," Sue repeated. "Why don't you sling up those two bags the way he said and be a pilot instead."

"All right." Grumpily, he did as she asked. "But I still say something's screwy." He caught at her arm as she stepped back. "Coming into town this weekend?"

She paused, then smiled at him affectionately. "Probably. Be a sweet thing and see if you can get a reservation at the hotel for me."

"That's my girl!" Before she could protest, he had pulled her into a whirlwind embrace and kissed her upturned lips.

She pushed at his chest halfheartedly. "Hey, that's enough."

"I wanted to leave you something to remember," he said, grinning down at her. "Wait 'til the weekend when I can really concentrate on things."

"Women would be safer if you were kept on a leash."

"Who wants to be safe? See you later, honey."

He vaulted into the cabin of the plane and slammed the door securely. She returned his mocking salute before she pushed the button to lower the landing platform and set the plane afloat.

He taxied out into the river and finally took

off before she made her way up the ramp and onto the path.

A smile played around her lips as she thought of Cal's style of lovemaking. He was about as subtle in his approach as a baby elephant, but what he lacked in finesse was compensated for by dogged persistence. With his engaging personality and masculine good looks, he hadn't found it necessary to add any refinements to his technique for the chase. Instead, it was usually a case of selecting which feminine companion he wanted for the moment from the multitude about him.

She almost collided with Nick at the bend of the path above the boathouse. "Heavens, you startled me! I didn't expect to see you again so soon."

"Sorry—I didn't mean to intrude." Obviously he was referring to Cal's farewell embrace and she noted his manner had become as impassive as a Coldstream guard on palace duty. "He should have chosen a more secluded place."

"I didn't mean that . . ." her words faltered, "I was talking about the luggage. What happened to it?"

"Marie met me halfway down the path with a cart. I came back to pick up the last two pieces. She said to tell you that she'll serve coffee in the lounge until you assign the rooms."

"In other words, she thinks I'd better get up

there." She assayed a smile which faded before his frigid expresssion. Deliberately, she made her voice as dispassionate as his. "Don't forget to bone up on that fishing information."

"I'll do it as soon as I get to the lodge." Translated, that remark meant that he'd get to the lodge a lot sooner if she would vacate the middle of the path.

Sue frowned. Was this the same man who teased her over breakfast just an hour ago? She gazed up at him and then dropped her eyes in honest bewilderment, her long lashes looking like feathery crescents on her pale cheeks.

For a moment, Nick's glance softened until he remembered Cal Martin's leavetaking and the stiffness came back. "If you'll excuse me, Miss Strathern . . . I have work to do," he began.

Her head jerked back as his impatient words penetrated. There was no reason for him to treat her like a slow learner. She decided that two could fight in this verbal battle.

"One moment please, Mr. Dunbar," her words fell between them like sharp pieces of ice. "I'll expect you to help entertain the guests as well as attending to your outside duties. That means you'll take your meals with us in the dining room no matter what your personal feelings are in the matter. I'm sorry if this will be distasteful, but we all have to make some sacrifices—even you."

With that ultimatum, she wheeled and disappeared up the path before Nick could open his mouth to reply. From the stormy look clouding his features, that reply would undoubtedly have been a dilly.

Her angry temper sustained itself through the coffee session in the lounge. As the minutes passed, it banked down to a steady glow of indignation against itinerant caretakers in general, and Wickitak's in particular. Who would have thought he'd add unpaid chaperon to his other duties? It served her right for ignoring written references and being taken in by a pleasant deep voice and piercing gray eyes.

She emerged from her thoughts to smile passably when Monica told how "quaint" it was to see a big, shaggy dog again—even an untrained one. The smile remained fixed when Leo pointed out with some asperity that he was violently allergic to all kinds of fleas. She merely said, "What a coincidence ... Rock is too!" without choking audibly on her words.

Florence decided to cut in quickly. "You worry too much, Leo," she said from where she sat in an overstuffed chair by the window. Her short legs barely reached the floor as she made herself comfortable on the big, down-filled cushion.

"Naturally I worry—that's why I have ulcers," Leo said defiantly. His pudgy hand toyed with the cup and saucer on the table beside him. "I hope the cook will remember that I can't take coffee. Just weak tea at all meals."

"Marie is good at remembering things," Sue assured him. "If you'll make a list of the forbidden foods on your diet, she can plan the menus around it."

"Monica can furnish you with stacks of lists," Leo's aunt said dryly.

The brunette glanced over from her stance by the window. "As soon as I unpack," she said.

Sue rose thankfully to the cue. "I'll take you up to your rooms now if you like. Lunch will be served at one o'clock." She noted raindrops starting to pelt against the windows. "Perhaps we'd better wait and see what the weather's like before making plans for the afternoon." Her gesture took in the lowering clouds. "September in southeast Alaska can be dreary."

Monica stared across the channel where the sharp contours of the clay hillside looked as if they had been edged by Paul Bunyan's ax. "Dead is a better word than dreary for this place," she said acidly. "I should have brought my knitting."

"I warned you," Leo taunted as he glanced across at Sue. "No eskimos or igloos ... no dog sleds?"

She shook her head and said flatly, "No eskimos, igloos, or dog sleds. Just bears and wolves and sometimes so much rain that you think you'll wash away. By the end of a week of it, you'll probably wish you had. But then..." her voice softened... "then you wake up the next morning and find it's clear. You step outside and take a deep breath of lovely cold, crisp air that feels as if it were delivered off the icecap especially for you. And suddenly you know that, with all its faults, this is the most marvelous land ever created."

"Hear... hear," Florence applauded. "That puts you in your place, Leo." She heaved herself erect. "Look at the bright side. Instead of worrying about fleas, just consider that this lovely air may clear up your sinus trouble. Now, let's get up to our rooms. Frankly, I can't wait to unpack my gouges and mallet so I can get to work." Sue's startled look caused her to chuckle. "I'm a wood carver, my dear, and my fingers are itching to start in on one of those chunks of cedar."

"We have plenty of raw material," Sue assured her. "Mr. Dunbar can find a piece for you. Now—if you'll follow me, I'll show you up to your suite. Your luggage should be up there by now."

She led them through the dining room and out into the entrance hall. Muted music from behind the kitchen door plus the smell of tomato and oregano proclaimed that Marie was in residence and spaghetti sauce was simmering for lunch. The probability that spaghetti sauce was on Leo's forbidden list lurked in Sue's mind as they went up the curving stairs. While she was showing the three-room suite at the end of the corridor, she was deciding how she could tactfully ask Marie to prepare a second entree. It was either that or they could all switch to omelets and junket for the duration.

"My dear—the rooms are lovely!" Florence's appreciative tones finally penetrated. "I can't imagine anyone not being comfortable here. Wickitak certainly deserves its reputation."

"Thank you, I hope you'll enjoy your stay." Through an open door, Sue noted Leo had unstrapped his bag and was busily lining medicine bottles up on his bureau. Monica had disappeared into her room without another word. "My room is at the head of the stairs if you should want me for anything," Sue reminded Florence as she left. Halfway down the corridor, her steps faltered. The thought of peace and quiet in her bedroom was undeniably attractive, but she should go down and warn Marie of Leo's list.

"Miss Strathern!"

The imperious call froze Sue by her bedroom door. Monica advanced down the hall brandishing a piece of paper. "Mr. Davis' diet—it's quite explicit."

"Thank you. I was going down to tell Marie," Sue reached for it, hoping to escape as quickly as possible from the secretary's superior gaze, "as soon as I get something from my bedroom." She reached for the doorknob behind her and fumbled in midair. Her hand connected with something that abruptly froze all movement. Since when had carved doors been covered in flannel? She revolved slowly to find the door standing wide open and Nick's broad shoulders taking up most of the frame.

Her instructions to him regarding the fishing information on the desk in the study came back vividly as they stood there in arrested motion. He was scowling slightly; probably at her for getting him involved in this mess, Sue decided.

"How cosy," Monica purred finally. "Imagine my thinking it was dull up here. There are all sorts of ... affairs ... going on, aren't there?"

Her arch look lingered long after her graceful figure undulated back down the hall.

It was the same expression which can be seen on numerous cats' faces each spring—as they carefully wash the baby bird feathers from their whiskers.

Chapter Three

Despite Monica's predilection for casting Sue as a modern Gold Rush camp follower, lunch went off amazingly well. During the meal most of the secretary's barbed conversational shafts were neatly turned aside and fell to the ground without scoring.

Florence was full of enthusiasm for everything north of the fiftieth parallel. "The people up here are perfectly charming," she emphasized over coffee later in the lounge. "So helpful—they go out of their way to make you feel welcome. Now take Mr. Martin, for example . . ."

"I think Miss Strathern already has," Monica drawled. "Taken him to her heart, I mean . . . such an attractive man."

"You must call me Sue," said the target of her remark. "In this *cosy* atmosphere, we don't stand on ceremony."

By the fireplace, Nick made a strangling sound as he swallowed some coffee. "Sorry," he apologized, noting the attention he had drawn, "something went down the wrong way."

The humorous glance he directed at Sue wasn't lost on Monica.

"Sue, then," the secretary said obligingly. "I've been admiring your outfit." She appraised the other's rust suede skirt and matching leather-trimmed beige cardigan. "Remarkably up-to-date for this part of the world."

"Thanks very much." Sue brushed an imaginary crumb from her cuff. "Actually I bought this in New York last month, but I saw a similar outfit in Juneau so I needn't have bothered."

"You see, Monica—I told you there was no need to fuss about clothes." Leo looked up triumphantly from where he was pouring a second cup of tea. His mood had improved tremendously since lunch, where he had consumed three helpings of spaghetti with a special spiceless sauce.

Sue made another mental note to raise Marie's wages immediately.

Leo went on, "The only thing that's different about this place is that they have the most terrific fishing in the world. I heard that the silvers are running now. How's the bottom out there in the channel?"

"The bottom?" Under the pretense of taking a sip of coffee, Sue tried to think what Uncle Tim had ever said about the bottom of the channel over the years. "It's just fine ... I think. Did you know ..." she tried to inject some enthusiasm in her tone, "that years ago the Alaskan halibut-fisherman used to test the bottom with balls of butter?"

Leo couldn't have looked more perplexed if she had gone into a buck and wing routine on the hearth. "No kidding! That sure seems the hard way to do it." He scratched his head. "But I don't go out for halibut."

"I think Sue wanted you to know some of the historical background around here," Nick said, breaking in quickly. "Actually you don't have to worry about bottom conditions; the cohos are striking pretty much at all depths. Herring and large spoons are the best bets."

"Fine!" Leo settled back contentedly on the couch. "I might try my Canadian Wonder Number 7. It's supposed to be the real thing for kings so it might work for cohos too."

Sue let out her breath in a soft sigh of relief. Her only interest in fish began and ended with their appearance on a plate in front of her, so it was fortunate that Nick had memorized his homework. It was almost worth that embarrassing session with Monica. His pleasant company manners during lunch indicated that he was momentarily willing to forget their altercation on the path, but after intercepting a few dark glances, she was aware that the truce was strictly temporary.

"What do you think about going out this afternoon?" Leo asked.

"I want to check out the engine on the

cruiser first," Nick told him, "but I can do that another day and we can go out in the dinghy instead."

"An open boat in this weather?" Leo sounded disgusted as he waved an indolent hand toward the windows where the rain was pelting down. "I'm not going out of my way to catch pneumonia."

"You don't catch pneumonia from getting a little bit wet," Monica put in.

"You catch pneumonia your way," Leo told her sourly, "I'll do it mine. My schedule for rainy weather doesn't include open boats. Maybe some gin rummy?" He looked hopefully at Monica.

"You'll have to find another partner because I plan to hitch a ride on the cruiser with Nick," Monica said calmly. "I'm pretty good help on a boat . . . tell him, Leo."

"She's not bad." Leo looked irritated at her independence. "How about you, Flo? Are you game for some gin rummy?"

"Only for a half hour or so. After that, I plan to work on the pattern for my carving. Nick's promised to find a piece of cedar in the dimensions I'll need."

"Right after I check out that engine," he promised.

"With my help," Monica added mischievously. She noted his questioning glance at Sue. "You don't mind do you, Miss Strathern?"

"Not at all," Sue said coolly. "Of course, all guests are required to wear a life jacket...."

"I'm an excellent swimmer...."

"At all times," Sue finished calmly, ignoring Monica's interruption. "Sorry, but that's the rule of the house. Even the best of swimmers can find themselves in trouble in this icy water. We also have floating hazards in the bergs from the glaciers and the occasional deadheads we get from log booms."

"Oh, all right," Monica capitulated with a flounce. "I'll go up and get ready." She eyed Nick. "Is nylon rain-gear acceptable under that life jacket?"

He grinned. "Nylon rain-gear is a fine idea. We'll try to find a life jacket to match it."

Sue banged her coffee mug down on the tray harder than she had anticipated. Rock, who was lying at her feet, winced at the unexpected noise and gave her a wounded look. One paw tightened protectively over the miniature rubber baseball bat he had brought into the lounge.

Sue bestowed an apologetic pat on his head. "Everything's all right. You can go back to sleep."

Monica stood up gracefully. "I'll see you later down in the boathouse, Nick," she promised before she disappeared through the doorway.

He nodded and then strolled over to put his

empty mug by the coffee urn. Pausing by Florence's side, he said "I'll have that cedar for you in a couple of hours."

"Fine, Nick. I can't wait to get started."

He flicked a casual glance at Sue. "Thanks for the coffee."

She was examining a cuticle carefully. "You're very welcome." Without lifting her head, she knew he was sending another of those impassive glances her way before he left the room.

Florence helped herself to more coffee. "If you want to play gin, Leo, you'd better find a deck of cards."

"We have some in that cabinet at the end of the bar," Sue said.

"I'll get them." Leo transferred his cup and saucer to a game table under the window and went over to the bar.

"You mustn't mind Monica, my dear," Florence said gently as Sue hovered by the end of the couch. "She collects gentlemen friends the way other people collect postage stamps, but you don't need to worry. Her interest doesn't last long."

Such solicitude, however well meant, rubbed against the grain of Sue's pride. She managed a stiff smile. "Thanks for your warning—I'll remember it if she ever approaches any of my gentlemen friends." The smile became warmer. "Fortunately, they're mostly in New York, so I won't have to build any fences."

Florence beamed appreciatively. "Of course not. A pretty girl like you wouldn't have any problems anyway." She evidently decided a change of subject was both necessary and desirable. "I had no idea that your uncle's property was so extensive." She motioned toward the map by the fireplace. "It must be extremely valuable."

"The timber rights might be," Sue temporized, "although Uncle Tim prefers to leave the land in its natural state. Those treeless patches always look pathetic to me—as if someone had slipped with a big electric clipper."

Florence nodded. "I feel that way too. It's a pity to have the ecology upset."

"In this case, though, you can't make that blanket declaration," Sue qualified. "Alaska needs a healthy economy, and industries like the pulp mills help to provide it. They, in turn, can't operate without the western hemlock and the Sitka spruce on our hillsides. That's their business. However, my uncle believes that running a hunting and fishing lodge is *his* business and he handles his property accordingly." She walked over to the map. "You can see that most of his land up by the glacier is pretty inaccessible. The difficulties in logging it would probably make the cost prohibitive. Just like Uncle Tim's gold-mining operation."

Leo's nose came up like an alert bird dog. "I didn't know there was mining around here."

"*Was* is the proper word—the gold mining's strictly past tense. With the price of gold fixed by the government, it isn't economically feasible to operate the mines around here. That's why the big one in Juneau closed during World War II and didn't reopen."

Leo sat down at the game table with a grimace of disgust. "I thought we could try our luck and stir up a little excitement."

"You can go look at our tunnel and try to find the vein," Sue told him. "The excitement comes if you meet a bear face-to-face while you're in there."

"That wasn't what I had in mind," he mumbled as he shuffled the cards.

"Don't be a spoilsport," Florence chided him. "I'd like to see the tunnel . . . it should be very interesting."

"We'll have a picnic lunch up there if the weather improves," Sue promised.

"I thought I was going fishing," Leo said.

"Let's plan for the day after tomorrow," she said diplomatically. "We can manage it in the forenoon and still get you back in plenty of time for your trip to Glacier Bay. It's a short flight and Mr. Martin can pick you up in the early afternoon."

"Fine!" Florence exclaimed. She turned to Leo. "Now—all that you have to do is catch one of those big salmon so we can have it for dinner tomorrow night and everything will be perfect."

He was dealing the cards. "There's no problem to that if Dunbar knows where to fish." He looked at Sue. "I suppose he's had plenty of experience?"

"I'm sure you'll find him satisfactory." She crossed her fingers behind her skirt as she spoke. From what she had heard of this year's coho run, Leo could catch fish if he dangled his toes in the water, but there was no use telling him that.

"Nicholas isn't your regular guide, is he?" Florence probed delicately. "Marie was telling us about her husband's accident on our flight up here."

"Joe is our usual guide, but Mr. Dunbar is a very old friend of the family and a splendid outdoorsman." Sue kept her fingers crossed, feeling intuitively that a small white lie in this case would certainly be better than the truth.

"He'd better be able to catch fish," Leo grumbled.

"Pay no attention to my nephew," Florence said fondly as she sat down opposite him. "He'll be in a much better humor after he beats me at gin rummy."

"Then I'll leave you to your game. If you'd like anything from the bar, please help yourselves." She picked up the coffee things and put them on the tray. "I'll see you later, but don't hesitate to buzz for Marie if you want something special in the meantime."

Leo's only acknowledgment was a jerk of his head, but Florence said, "How thoughtful! I wish we'd made arrangements to stay longer here at Wickitak."

Sue's responsive smile didn't quite reach her eyes as she made her way into the dining room with the tray. Discounting Florence's determined good humor, catering to the other two members of her party and one caretaker already indicated a need to throttle frequent homicidal urges. With luck, she might manage to avoid any further encounters with Monica and Nick until cocktail time.

"And the cocktail hour should be enough to give me indigestion for the rest of the night," she informed Rock, who was plodding along beside her. "Monica will probably appear in a glamorous creation that will get every smidgen of attention." There was no use explaining whose attention Monica would attract as Rock suddenly veered off in the direction of the kitchen door.

The writing of a determinedly cheerful letter to Uncle Tim helped soothe her disposition for the rest of the afternoon. She couldn't resist adding a postscript, which said "I don't see why you had to go all the way to east Africa to look at the animals when we have such a collection here. Compared to some of the inmates occupying our best suite, even a timber wolf would look good."

A vision of Monica in wolf's clothing seemed amazingly appropriate, and it still lingered as Sue pulled on her best black sheer wool for the cocktail session. She stepped into black velveteen pumps and gazed into the mirror. Her reflection stared back, looking apathetic and wan. "Like a refugee who's been on a hunger strike," she muttered, changing the shade of her lipstick to a more vibrant red.

The change in lipstick helped. So did the decision to style her hair in a sophisticated French roll. The final touch came with a pair of jade earrings and a jade clip on the shoulder of her dress. It was a new costume for hunting bear, she decided, as she dabbed Carven's Ma Griffe on the inside of her wrists and descended the stairs in an aromatic haze which made Rock's nose twitch when she reached him at the bottom.

"Cocktail time, my friend," she announced. "If you're a good dog, you might get an ice cube."

He followed happily in her wake.

The guests hadn't needed a gong to proclaim that cocktails were being served. Nick, in a gray suit and immaculate white shirt, had evidently been pressed into service as chief bartender. He glanced up as she paused in the doorway.

For an instant, his look was hard to fathom and then seeing her slight frown, he merely said "Good evening, would you like something to drink?"

Monica swung round on the bar stool in front of him. "Hello there, Sue. I hope you don't mind that we went ahead without you. Nick and I were parched after being out on the boat."

"Of course not." Sue's answer was automatic, her eyes slipping over the other's outfit and mentally throwing up her hands in total surrender.

Monica had donned a sheer slate-blue chiffon blouse which draped in all the right places and some of the wrong ones. Below it, pleated silk organza trousers in a blue and purple print swirled gracefully around her ankles. The outfit was about as appropriate for dinner at Wickitak as wearing a bikini for breakfast in the Aleutians, but no one could deny that it was eye-catching.

Beside her, Sue felt her sheer wool looked as provocative as a sealskin parka.

She sighed and edged up on a stool next to Leo, who was consuming champagne from a large bottle on the bar. "Is that for sharing, Mr. Davis?"

"Sure thing ... but make it Leo," he said genially and signaled for another glass. "Help yourself. It's the only thing for a nervous stomach."

"Do you have a nervous stomach, Sue?" Monica asked sweetly.

"Not yet ... but I'm working on it." She noticed that Nick had retrieved his highball glass and was relaxing against the back of the bar. "Rock would appreciate it if you'd let any extra ice cubes slip to the floor."

His slow smile brought his features to life. "I wondered why he was sitting so patiently by my feet."

"How did the cruiser go?" she asked.

"Marvelously," Monica cut in. "Nick was wonderful handling it. We hated to come back."

"I can imagine. . . ."

"Beats me why you wanted to go out in this downpour in the first place," Leo said truculently. "I didn't know we'd arrive in the monsoon season."

"Oh, it isn't bad at Wickitak," Sue said. "On Baranof Island, they get two hundred-twenty inches a year. By comparison, we're in the banana belt."

He shuddered and poured more champagne.

"It's supposed to clear tomorrow," she said, relenting. "You should have a good day for fishing."

Leo became enthusiastic for the first time.

"Fine! Maybe I'll have something to tell the guys back at the office, after all."

"Where is your business located?" Nick asked casually.

"Our main branch is in Chicago," Leo said, leaning on the bar, "so I can get a little fishing in on Lake Michigan when I have the time. Nothing like this, of course."

"Ah, there you are!" Florence's brisk voice from the doorway caused them to look around quickly.

As Nick saw the good-sized piece of cedar she was carrying, he hurriedly put down his glass and went over to take it from her.

"How kind of you," she told him gratefully. "I hope you don't mind my bringing it into the lounge, Sue. I thought I'd look at it and see if a real inspiration would come ... for my carving pattern, I mean."

The perplexed lines on Sue's forehead eased. "Now I understand. For a minute, I thought you were being subtle and indicating the furnace thermostat wasn't set high enough."

Florence chuckled. "Of course not. Nick—if you'd just put it here on the table by the fireplace ... thank you very much." She sank onto the davenport by it. "Now, a glass of sherry will keep me from collapsing right in front of you."

"Sweet or dry?"

"Dry, please." She arranged the skirt of her

unobtrusive charcoal knit dress and plumped a pillow behind her back.

"One dry sherry as ordered." Nick put the glass by her elbow.

"Lovely." She beamed up at him. "I'm just going to sit here—look at my piece of wood—and let inspiration come."

Sue noticed that although Leo and Monica looked profoundly bored by the woodcarving talk, they maintained a respectful silence as they turned back to their drinks. Evidently Florence was more important than a mere chaperon for them.

Nick had no sooner gotten behind the bar than a plaintive "Woof" floated up.

"Sorry, Rock." He reached obligingly for the ice bucket again. "I thought one was your limit."

"That animal is disgustingly spoiled," Monica proclaimed as she glanced sideways at Sue. "I'm surprised that your uncle allows it."

A furtive smile touched the other's lips. "He not only allows it . . . he's responsible for it. Over the years, Rock has acquired quite a following among Uncle Tim's guests, as well. They've seen him carrying things around in his mouth and usually bring a toy on their next visit. He has an impressive collection."

"I know," Monica said acidly. "I've been stumbling over it ever since I got here."

"I'll try to do better in keeping them picked

up," Sue said apologetically. "I think most big dogs create some clutter, though."

At that moment, Rock emerged from the back of the bar carrying a rubber baby doll in his mouth.

"I suppose that's normal for big dogs too," Monica said, drawing fastidiously aside.

Sue hurriedly removed the doll's head from the Airedale's mouth and offered him a foot to carry it by instead. "He doesn't hurt it," she explained, "he just likes to move it around."

"Pay no attention to Monica," Leo said comfortingly. He pushed his glasses up further on the bridge of his nose and peered through them at the dog and his dangling passenger. "God! I'm glad I saw that on my *first* bottle of champagne."

"When it's time for after-dinner liqueurs," Nick contributed, grinning, "we make sure he's shut up in the kitchen."

"A totem!" Florence suddenly proclaimed. "It cries out for a totem!"

"I beg your pardon," Sue said, wondering if she'd missed the first reel of something.

Florence waved her sherry glass. "I've decided," she announced, "I'll carve a totem."

Leo frowned. "You've only got a two-foot piece of wood."

"A *small* totem, then," she amended with some irritation. "Must you be so literal, Leo!"

"Uncle Tim has some splendid books on totem poles," Sue put in hastily. "I'll get them for you after dinner. There are also some fine examples of Indian art in Juneau's museum if you're interested."

"A fellow on the flight up here was going on about Indian stuff," Leo said, unabashed by his aunt's ill humor. "He knew I was interested in fishing and was telling me how the Indians in western Canada used to make their canoes. It seems they'd go out in the forest and find a cedar tree . . . then they'd cut two notches on one side of it after measuring off the length they wanted for their canoe." He gestured expansively with his glass. "After that, they just went back to their village and waited for a storm. Apparently the tree would bend in the high wind and the wood would split straight as a die between the notches. Practically 'instant canoe' . . . how about that?"

Nick nodded. "He must have been talking about the Haidas. There are a lot of those Indian legends floating around up here."

"And a lot of totem poles," Monica murmured. "Do you really think they need another one, Florence?"

"Really my dear, you don't understand artists. It will be the ideal thing to take home; I merely hope I can give it the proper significance."

"The only significance Alaskan totems had was social," Nick said. "Most people don't realize there was no religious connotation; they carved them to tell a story. The Indians had no written language, but their totems can be divided into broad general types. For example, there's a Potlatch Pole, which is usually the largest..." he broke off suddenly as he noted Sue's intent gaze. "I'm sure Miss Strathern could tell you better than I could."

"No—go on, Nick," Monica urged as Florence nodded agreement.

"Well, to make it short and sweet—you use the figures on the pole as sort of a memory device to recall a story and always read from the top down. The symbolism was generally the same; for example, they use the raven as a being of almost supernatural power. The eagle, which was another popular figure, always had its beak turned downward. That was to distinguish him from the hawk, which has the point of its beak turned back and touching its face."

There was a silence as his voice trailed off and then Monica murmured, "I had no idea those old poles were so interesting." She pushed a strand of silky hair behind her ear and went on, "I wonder what kind of figures those same carvers would use today?"

"Probably something similar," Sue said. "Times haven't changed so much around here. Florence will see that when she looks at the reference books." A gong sounded from the front hall and she glanced at her watch. "Dinner-time. Marie is serving buffet-style tonight. Take your drinks along to the table if you'd like."

Florence clutched her glass of sherry and moved toward the dining room. "You've given me so many wonderful ideas about those totems that I won't be able to concentrate on food."

"I will," Leo said definitely as he swallowed the last of his wine and slid off the bar stool. "I'm starving."

Monica put down her glass and then leaned over the bar to look intimately up into Nick's face. "Come on, Nicky—tell me what kind of figure those carvers would use for me."

It was hard to tell what was in his mind, but his tone was easy. "Let me think about it," he promised. "I'll tell you later on." He removed her glass from the bar top.

Monica pulled back with a satisfied smile. She glanced triumphantly over her shoulder at Sue and then moved leisurely away.

"More champagne?" Nick's words were noncommittal.

"No thanks. I think I've had too much already." Sue shoved her glass toward him. "At least, something's making me feel ill."

A surge of red appeared beneath his cheekbones. "Oh?"

"I had no idea you were such an expert on totems," she mimicked, disregarding that frosty monosyllable.

"There are lots of things you don't know about me." It was a flat statement of fact.

She scraped her bar stool back forcefully. "I'm learning. It's amazing what a paragon I hired from a one-inch newspaper ad: a trail cook, a wizard with boats, and now a crackerjack totem expert." She took a deep breath. "If you'd like some free advice, you can tell Monica that the signs for women like her were usually claws and beaks."

The virulent words hung in the air between them and suddenly she had an overwhelming urge to call them back, to apologize wholeheartedly for acting and sounding like a nasty shrew.

Nick's expression indicated he shared her feeling. "Thanks for your offer," he said dispassionately. "Don't forget the elevated snout and sharp teeth—they can double for a predator or any woman." He gave her a cold look. "Now, are we quits in this match?"

"Nicky—are you coming?" Monica's voice floated back. "I'm saving a place for you."

Sue made a noise that sounded suspiciously like a snort. His jaw tightened and he motioned her toward the other room.

She persisted in continuing the discussion. "Actually, Mr. Dunbar, you should stop off in Ketchikan and visit the totem display at Saxman. They have a fascinating pole which reminds me of you."

He stopped abruptly at the dining-room arch as if he had stumbled over a firecracker with a short, sputtering fuse. One eyebrow went up as he asked "All right, Mrs. Bones—I'll bite. Which pole should I see at Saxman?"

She was edging toward the buffet and he had to strain to hear her words. "Ask for the one called 'Tired Wolf'—there's a remarkable resemblance."

Chapter Four

After thinking it over through most of a sleepless night, Sue decided there were three courses open to her at breakfast the next morning: she could get Nick aside and apologize for her bad manners, she could treat him casually as if the entire episode had never happened, or she could stay out of his way and hope that she'd think of a better idea.

There was no need to flip a mental coin, she decided, creeping down the back stairs to the kitchen. Obviously the last idea was best as she was too much of a coward for the first and too poor an actress to carry off the second. The sensible thing would be to take a cup of coffee back up to her room and hide behind closed doors until the fishing expedition was out of the lodge. She could always make conversation with Florence after the others were gone. The older woman had found a place by the back porch to put her cedar log and planned to spend the entire day "creating," as she called it, while Leo and Monica went with Nick.

Sue ran an impatient hand through her hair as she passed a wall mirror. Even the royal blue of her favorite turtleneck sweater didn't do much to improve her sleepless pallor. Oh well ... Marie wouldn't comment on it and she could add more makeup to look less like a terminal case before the fishermen returned.

She pushed through the swinging door at the back of the kitchen. "Good morning, Marie—the coffee smelled so good that I thought I'd ..." Her voice trailed off as she saw the sole occupant of the room was a tall figure leaning nonchalantly against the draining board.

"Good morning," Nick said. "Marie will be back in a minute. She went out to her apartment for something." He gestured toward the coffeepot. "Would you like a cup?"

"I can manage, thanks." She became suddenly aware of the scruffy look of her corduroy slacks and wished that she'd stifled the urge for prebreakfast exploring. It obviously wasn't possible to do an about-face and disappear back up the stairs, as much as she'd like to. She tugged at her sweater to give it a semblance of chic and went over to get a mug from the cupboard. "I didn't expect to see you down so early."

"That's obvious, but even wolves get hungry." If she'd looked up, she would have seen the flicker of humor pass over his features. "Especially tired ones," he explained.

"Oh stop it—darn you!" She whirled, almost spilling hot coffee onto her hand in the process. "I was going to apologize ... later on."

"I should certainly hope so."

Rock chose that moment to stumble sleepily into the kitchen. He stared at them with glazed brown eyes, stretched laboriously, and yawned—emitting a strange squeak at the end of it. Then, as if completely exhausted by his activities, he struggled over behind the stove and collapsed.

"My lord! Is he all right?" Nick wanted to know.

"Of course. Rock isn't at *his* best until noon and I have *my* mad moments at dinner. I'm paying for my sins, though. My atrocious behavior gave me insomnia. That's why I'm up so early."

"I'm sorry you had a rotten night." There was evidently something of great interest in the bottom of his coffee mug. "The thing that made me the maddest was your conviction that I was going to collapse at Monica's feet. I should have told you that I hadn't been out in the bush that long."

She flushed but admitted, "The way Monica looks, she could collect her limit in Times Square or the North Pole without any difficulty."

"If you like the obvious kind."

Feeling unaccountably relieved, she looked over at him through narrowed lashes. "Far be it from me to defend her," she began and stopped as he broke out laughing.

"That would be a switch." He put his coffee

mug on the table. "Sure you don't want to come along on the fishing trip after breakfast?"

"Quite sure, thanks." She smiled. "That would tempt my good humor too far. Besides, I'm a miserable fisherman."

He nodded. "Then you might as well go back to bed and make up some of that sleep you lost. Later on, I'd like you to keep an eye on the generator ... the motor's been sounding sick."

"I'll check," she promised. "If you need any parts, Cal can fly them in or Captain Fergus can bring them on the mail boat."

"We'll see. It will probably be all right."

"Do you have any qualms about the trip today?"

"No, the cruiser's easy enough to handle and your uncle has all the charts in good order." He added before she could say anything, "Don't worry, I know enough to be careful in the trickier currents and watch for floating ice."

"I didn't think you planned to go flat out down the middle of the channel, but you do have to be cautious in these waters. There's always the ship-to-shore radio if you get in real trouble."

"Don't worry, we'll be all right. Monica may act like a featherbrain most of the time, but she has been around boats." He shoved his hands in the pockets of light blue denims. "Once Leo gets his hands on a fishing pole, the only problem will be getting him back to shore."

"Try to make it in time to clean the fish," she urged with a grin. "I think Marie's planning on baked salmon."

"If the entree turns out to be peanut butter sandwiches, I'll eat in my room. But don't forget, lunch tomorrow at the mining shaft's on you. My trail cooking stops short at ham and eggs."

She cocked her head to one side. "You know, I don't altogether believe you, Mr. Dunbar."

"We're suitably acquainted by now," he growled. "You can drop that 'Mr. Dunbar' stuff for once and for all."

"All right ... provided 'Miss Strathern' goes with it. You've made me feel like a maiden aunt."

"I've never seen anyone look less like one."

Her throat tightened at his whimsical glance and for the moment, the only sound in the kitchen was Rock's stertorous breathing. When Marie's footsteps sounded outside, they both moved abruptly as if a tableau had come to life.

"All right." Sue tried to calm her chaotic thoughts and remember what they had been talking about. "The picnic lunch is on me." She cleared her throat. "I can always make an extra platter of peanut butter sandwiches."

"If that's your menu, I'll have words with Marie. Remember, you were the one who threatened dire things if I didn't eat with you." His eyes glinted with devilment. "The temporary caretakers' union has a rule against peanut butter sandwiches for lunch—it's all right for employers and guests, but the employees need more variety." He enjoyed her obvious confusion for a moment before he nodded gently in the direction of the stairs. "Get back up there and go to sleep, little one. Have a good day."

She must have gotten up the stairs somehow but later she couldn't remember touching the steps. When she closed her bedroom door, she stood leaning against it. It was a pity to go back to sleep when she was having the most wonderful dream of her life without closing her eyes.

There was the slam of a door from the suite and then the sound of a feminine voice in the hall. Sue's smile deepened. Even if Monica's angling had a twofold purpose during the day, she was apt to be disappointed in landing her catch on this trip.

Fortunately for Wickitak's reputation, the weather continued fair. Even the salmon cooperated and Leo spoke of making annual visits to Alaska when he came in tired and happy after his day on the cruiser. Monica's mood was difficult to assess, so Sue decided to ignore it. Florence was the only one of the three who looked decidedly petulant.

"It's my totem," she confessed after a morning of pattern tracing and an afternoon of making chips on the back porch. "My beaver is awful . . . his front teeth don't match and his tail looks like a canoe paddle."

"Don't be discouraged," Sue said comfortingly. "Totems are difficult even for professionals. Perhaps you should concentrate on the decorative feathers at the base for a beginning."

"That's an idea," the other murmured, as she gathered up her gouges and the lethal-looking mallet. "I could start on a border of feathers after we get back from Glacier Bay—there won't be time tomorrow morning if we're going to visit that mining shaft."

"Well—it *is* quite a hike with the jeep out of commission."

Florence nodded. "I daresay it will be good for us to have the exercise." She looked ruefully down at her plump hips and then at Sue's sleek figure. "It just isn't fair," she moaned.

Sue smiled in sympathy. "Don't start dieting until tomorrow. Marie's baked salmon is too good to miss."

Of Nicholas, there was only a fleeting glimpse in the late afternoon. He had delivered the cleaned salmon to the kitchen and leveled a slow smile at Sue, who was concentrating on a dill-bread recipe. After announcing that he'd be washing down the cruiser for the next hour or so, he went out whistling. Sue could only surmise that his self-imposed task was preferable to making conversation with their guests. The thought was so cheering that she almost forgot to put softened yeast in her bread dough.

The sun was still shining bravely the next forenoon when the party assembled by the boathouse for their outing to the mine shaft. Dense shrubs of fireweed and salmonberry lined the edge of the dirt track by the building and provided shelter for the delicate mosses covering the ground at their roots. Behind them, bright drops of dew lined the fleecy branches of the hemlocks and the tall, sturdy trunks of the Sitka spruce.

"Everything's so damp!" Monica shuddered gently and turned up the collar of her quilted, red nylon jacket.

"Well, it *is* September and this part of Alaska *is* a rain forest," Sue told her, "but the sun should stay out long enough for us to have lunch. Let's see if we have everything we need; Florence, you're carrying the thermos bag...."

The older woman, in sturdy hiking shoes and a serviceable tweed outfit, looked up from her contemplation of the berrylike fruit of the salal and waved the leather-cased thermos agreeably. "I was wishing I'd remembered to put in a sketching pad, but I can do that another time."

Sue nodded and went on. "Nick and Leo have the knapsacks with the food...."

The two men were deep in conversation by the carport end of the boathouse and didn't bother to look up. Both were dressed in rugged outdoor clothing and wore laced hiking boots. It was amazing the difference a change in clothing effected in Leo's personality; he seemed to gather stature and inches once he shed that rumpled business suit.

Sue continued her checkoff. "Monica..."

"Monica is carrying nothing but her own sweet self," that young lady said definitely.

"There's no need." Sue took a last look around. "I have the binoculars and the camera ... so that's everything. We can put them in the knapsack once the food is gone."

A bloodcurdling howl split the air as she spoke and Monica started nervously.

"Wolves!" she gasped. "I'm not going out in...."

"Wolves hell!" Leo interrupted. "It's that dog!"

"I had to shut Rock in the lodge when he wanted to come," Sue explained. "I didn't want him to be a nuisance to you."

"Thank heaven for some small favors," Monica said waspishly, undoubtedly feeling foolish after her startled outburst, "but I do think we should have some kind of gun along."

"The only things we'd be apt to meet at this

time of day would be black bears," Nick told her, "and they'll get out of your way. Just make the normal amount of noise and don't creep up on them."

"Do you think I'm crazy?" Obviously Monica needed no such strictures.

At the end of the carport, Leo was peering under an old army tarp covering the jeep. "Why aren't we riding in this?"

"Because it won't go," Sue said ruefully. "Joe had removed a part when he went off to the hospital. By the time I could get delivery on a new one, he'll be back to replace the original."

Leo replaced the tarp with a snort of disgust.

Monica moved over to inspect some equipment hanging from pegs on the carport wall. "What's all this stuff, Nicky?"

"It's climbing gear. I imagine Mr. Strathern keeps it around for ice work on the glacier." Nick gave Sue a questioning glance. She nodded and he turned back to Monica. "Those metal things with the straps are crampons that you put over your boot soles for traction; the oval rings are carabiners to link yourself to your climbing rope. And of course, these are ice axes. Among other things, you can use them for self-arrest if you fall crossing the glacier."

"Uncle Tim has quite a few guests who are interested in climbing," Sue contributed. "The rough glacier ice holds a particular fascination for them." Her smile was rueful. "I can testify from experience that Alaskan glaciers aren't for beginning climbers."

Leo stalked impatiently out into the open. "Let's get moving—I want to be back in time for our flight this afternoon. Even if I'm not interested in climbing any of the damned glaciers, I would like to see those in Glacier Bay. Frankly, they sound a lot more interesting than an abandoned gold shaft."

Sue fell into step beside him as they went down the track. "There is some pretty country on the way to it, though. The trail goes along the shore and you'll see the difference in our ground cover; cottonwood and wild crab-apple trees down there, alder up on the avalanche zones, and lodgepole pine in the muskeg."

Florence came alongside, leaving Nick and Monica to bring up the rear. Sue risked a glance over her shoulder and then turned back quickly as Nick gave her a slow wink.

"What's muskeg?" Leo was asking.

"It's another word for bog area," Sue explained. "We skirt one on the beginning of the trail up to the shaft. If you'd like, we can take a few minutes off and harvest some Labrador tea while we're there."

"Is that a cousin of orange pekoe?"

"Very distant. This is a shrub found in the marshes around this part of the state. The leaves are strongly aromatic and can be thrown in boiling water to make tea if you're short on provisions."

"We could have some for lunch," Florence said enthusiastically.

"Just a little. To much could cause . . ." Sue sought for a suitable adjective " . . . intestinal disturbances."

Leo crowed with laughter before his aunt could quell him with a look. "In that case," she said with dignity, "I'll be happy to just look at the plant."

"Of course," Sue soothed. "Actually some of the plants up here can be quite lethal unless you're familiar with them. Take the false hellebore, which is found on the low ground in this area—it's often fatal to sheep and other animals."

Monica was listening to their conversation. "My god!" she said, aghast. "This nature walk gets worse and worse." She stopped in the middle of the path. "I'm going back."

Nick put a hand at her elbow and urged her forward. "Don't worry, I supervised the packing of our lunch myself. Nothing more lethal than roast beef sandwiches and apple turnovers for dessert. Not a stalk of false hellebore in the lot."

She let herself be led forward, grumbling. "How far is it to this miserable hole in the hill?"

"Not far," Sue assured her. "We'll be there in good time for lunch."

When they finally arrived at the abandoned mine shaft, Monica sat down on a fallen log by the entrance and refused to stir further. She watched Nick and Leo haul away the timbers propped in front of the A-shaped opening to keep trespassers away. "I should think your uncle would put up more of a barrier," she told Sue as the latter dug in a knapsack for a flashlight. "A determined pygmy could move those logs."

"Well, this isn't a main highway and there is a 'Danger—Keep Out' sign over the entrance."

"I saw that first thing and intend to follow it to the letter. I haven't the slightest intention of setting foot in that dark hole."

"Actually, I don't blame you," Sue told her. "It gives me the willies too. We won't be long."

She moved into the opening after carefully flashing the beam of her light around the tunnel area just inside the entrance. "I think we can all get in here," she told the others and moved against the rocky side of the aperture to let them sidle by. "Watch that you don't touch those supporting timbers. Uncle Tim put them in a few years ago after there had been some avalanches on this part of the hillside and they've weakened the ground cover." She looked uneasily over their heads. "After the heavy rain of this past summer, I'd hate to shift that bracing."

"We'll be careful, dear," Florence promised, looking with interest along the shaft to where the tunnel narrowed and wound out of sight in the hard rock. "I suppose this was hacked out years ago?"

"Yes—by pickax and hand drill. There weren't any jackhammers or compressed air drills to bore holes for the dynamite in those days."

Florence ran inquisitive fingers along the sharp-edged rock and nodded. "It was a hard life but that's the way miners have had it all through history. The Greek historian Diodorus tells how Egyptian slaves worked in the Pharaoh's gold tunnels with candles strapped to their heads. And if you think Alaskan miners found things difficult with their pickaxes, just remember that in Siberia, the men had to crawl through small tunnels and scrabble away at the gold quartz with tools pointed by boar's fangs. Gmelin wrote of that."

"You've evidently read a lot about gold mining," Nick said.

The older woman's face was shadowed as she turned toward him, but her voice was clear. "Women have always been interested in gold, Nick." A thread of humor underlined her words. "Gold has meant power right down through the ages. Look at the stories in the

Bible; the gold for the Ark of the Covenant, Romans paying out gold to the barbarians to keep from being pillaged. The Aztecs, the Incas—with their whole history changed because of the precious metal." Her hand stroked the cold rock wall almost sensuously. "As far as I'm concerned, these old tunnels tell the most fascinating stories in the world."

A silence followed her words. Somewhere in a far corner, water dripped onto the stone floor and then a small rush of gravel cascaded downward as Leo shifted against the far wall.

"If it's all the same to you," he told his aunt after looking around uneasily, "let's continue the story outside."

"Of course." Florence gave a final comprehensive glance at their surroundings and led the way back to the mine opening. "Forgive me for getting carried away," she said to Sue. "History was my favorite subject when I was teaching."

"Heavens, don't apologize. I want to hear some more at lunch."

"That's the topic I've been hoping someone would discuss." Nick took the flashlight from Sue as they went outside. "Where do we eat?"

"The question is 'when?'" Monica asked plaintively as she got up from the log and stretched.

"The answer is 'practically immediately,'" Sue assured her. "There's a clearing with a gorgeous view if we follow this path." She gestured to the right of the tunnel entrance. "Only about five minutes more and then luncheon is served."

Thick roast beef sandwiches consumed in a sunny mountain setting overcame all prejudices against September picnics even when their table was a broad tree stump and a fallen log the only place to sit.

Leo braved the bark under him through the sandwich course but decided to swallow the last bites of his apple turnover in a standing position. "Hey!" he looked at the thermos capful of coffee in his other hand. "It's starting to rain!"

Sue nodded in resignation. "I'm afraid so. Evidently we've finished our picnic just in time." She set about clearing the remains. "It won't take long to dispose of the garbage."

Nick slung a knapsack with the camera and binoculars in it onto his back. "I'll go down and put back the tunnel barricades."

"That's a good idea." Sue felt the rain develop into a steady drizzle on her shoulders. "If the rest of you want to go ahead, take the left fork and we'll catch up at the main path."

"That isn't the way we came," Florence protested.

"I know. It bypasses the path by the mine and saves some steps. If you're going to get back to the lodge by the time Cal arrives, you'd best take it."

No one needed further urging. The three disappeared under the now-dripping trees on the trail and Nick strode down the steeper path to the right.

Sue put the last napkins and sandwich wrappers in her lightened pack and then took a final look to make sure there was no remaining evidence of their midday meal. She started down the left-hand path only to pull up shortly after a few steps. Nick could probably use some help in replacing those timbers. Her eyes glinted with amusement as she thought it over. She could offer that as an excuse for joining him although it was as transparent as some of Monica's dodges.

She cut across to the other path and went carefully down the steep slope, her almost-empty pack bouncing against her back. The rain had set in for a steady downpour, but thready clouds were still allowing enough visibility for Cal to set down at Wickitak. She sneaked a glance at her watch. It was a good thing that her guests had already packed for their outing to Glacier Bay and that their bags were stacked by the boathouse ready to be transferred to the plane.

There was a rustle in the undergrowth to her left which died away as she froze to a startled stop. Then she took a deep breath and moved on; probably a curious bear or deer was hurriedly making tracks in the opposite direction.

The path broadened and leveled as it curved onto the ledge by the tunnel opening. Her quick glance took in the deserted clearing with Nick's bright orange knapsack thrown carelessly on the ground next to the mine entrance. Unconsciously, she noted that part of the timber barrier had been replaced; as if he had started his job before being interrupted in the middle of it.

She let her own knapsack slide off her shoulders as she cautiously approached the shaft opening. Carefully, she peered around the sagging timbers in the deserted tunnel and was about to turn away again when she heard the noise of rock falling in the distance.

"Nick?" Her voice was thin and uncertain as it echoed from the stone walls. She advanced another few steps into the dark shaft. Another sound from beyond the curve of the tunnel caused her to cup her hands and shout "Nick! Are you all right?"

"Is that you, Sue?" The answer was reassuringly normal. "Come on back—I'm in the side tunnel."

"All right . . . I'm on the way."

Partial light turned to murky darkness as the narrow tunnel twisted away from the entrance.

"Do you always examine things in the dark?" She felt her way until she finally caught sight of the flickering flame from his cigarette lighter and hurried to his side. "You had me scared to death."

"Sorry," he said absently. "I was curious to see the condition of this side tunnel."

"Ummm." She edged closer. "You and your curiosity. This place gives me the creeps."

"I'm sorry." She had his full attention now. "It isn't the most cheerful place in the world, is it?" His hand rested reassuringly on her shoulder. "Listen—you go on back to the entrance and wait outside. I'll only be a couple minutes more and then we'll catch up . . ."

The sudden crashing thud of collapsing timber swept away the sound of his voice and caused her to instinctively duck into his embrace until the noise died away.

His arms tightened for a moment and then he said calmly, "Come on, Sue—we'd better get back to the entrance and see if things are as bad as they sound."

He grasped her hand and used the wavering lighter flame to case a feeble light in the tunnel.

The Stygian black that greeted them in the main shaft provided part of the answer; the dust and dirt particles that hung in the air near the debris covering the entrance provided the rest.

"Damn . . . !" Nick's remark was understandably profane. He pulled her back from the still-shifting mass. "Let's wait here a few minutes until that's settled. Then I'll take a look and see if there's any way we can crawl out." He closed the top of his lighter ... extinguishing the flame and letting the black murk surround them.

He must have felt her gasp for he reached out to pull her into a comfortingly close embrace, but even the warmth of his hard body couldn't still the trembling of hers.

"Hey ... cut it out." His voice was close to her ear. "We'll get out of this all right, honey. Don't be scared."

Her head burrowed deeper into his shirt. "It's this miserable darkness. I think I've passed the point of being scared, Nick," She tried to laugh but it came out as a pathetic squeak. "I'm now approaching the state of absolute mortal terror."

Chapter Five

"Stop it, Sue!" Nick's words came from another world, but the hands gripping her shoulders were painfully real. "This is no time to pass out," he was saying. "Sit down—lean against the wall."

She felt her body being jackknifed onto the cold rock and her head pressed between her knees.

"Take a deep breath," he commanded.

She fought to sit upright. "I'm all right now. For a moment there ..." her husky voice trailed off and then she made another try, "I'm sorry ... I've always had a thing about small dark places."

His hand slid down her arm and gripped her wrist. "Then this must be hell for you. Look here—I can use the lighter...."

"No." She shook her head although she realized as she was doing it that it was a useless gesture in the dark. "Save it. We'll need it later."

"There's not much doubt about that." He moved from his crouching position to sit beside her; his back propped against the rough stone wall. "I gather our chums aren't going to start rescue operations from the outside."

"Not unless they can be in two places at once. They had a five-minute start down the other trail before I even took this path. Besides ..." a vestige of humor crept into her words for the first time ... "can you honestly see Leo or Monica ruining their manicures to dig us out?"

"Nope. They'd be more apt to take after Brutus with his 'I come to bury Caesar, not to praise him.' "

"Not only that but we'd interrupt their schedule. Cal is probably waiting at the boathouse right now and they'll take off without giving us a second thought."

"How about Cal? Won't he think it strange that you aren't there?"

"No ..." she drew out the monosyllable thoughtfully, "not if they told him I was up on the trail. In this weather, he can't afford to wait if he's to get them in to Glacier Bay." She sighed. "I might as well tell you the rest of the good news. Marie was going to ask him for a ride down to Juneau tonight so she could visit Joe. She won't be back on the mail boat until tomorrow morning. That means Cal won't know anything's wrong until I don't check in by radio tonight. It will be morning before any help arrives."

"If that's the case, we'd better get moving. I don't intend to wait," he said, pushing erect.

"Hold on, Nick." She reached up to catch at his trouser leg. "There's no use trying to shift that stuff at the entrance; you'll have the whole mountainside down on us. I was a fool to come this way today ... Uncle Tim's been worried about a cave-in here for years."

"It didn't look that bad," he said, trying to ease her obvious distress. "Besides, there wasn't any trouble until you came haring in after me."

"Carefully leaving my flashlight on the ground outside," she concluded bitterly.

"Never mind ... this lighter should help. Come on," he felt for her hand and hoisted her up beside him.

"What now?"

He spun the wheel on his lighter and let the flame flare up before he answered. "We're going out by the rear entrance."

She peered over at his shadowed face. "That was supposed to be my big surprise. How did you know about it?"

"I saw it on the map. Keep beside me...." He was protecting the flame with his cupped hand. "It's going to be tricky avoiding the side tunnels and I don't want to waste any time. Hang onto my belt if it's easier."

"You have about as much chance of losing me as shedding a second skin." She shuddered as grit sifted onto her face. "This is the stuff that nightmares are made of."

"Then let's get out of here."

The slow and tortuous journey through the old, abandoned shaft in the hours that followed called for every bit of Sue's self-control. Throughout the entire ordeal, there was the unspoken fear that the wavering flame of the lighter would disappear altogether leaving them trapped in the darkness. That thought became foremost in Sue's mind when they wasted time in side shafts which wound like fiendish mazes only to end abruptly and send them stumbling wearily back to look for the main tunnel. It was as unsafe to try to hurry as it was difficult to see the occasional holes in the tunneling beneath their feet. Only the careful placing of each foot saved them from pitching forward precipitously when they encountered one. On one such happening, the lighter had flown out of Nick's grasp and both of them had groveled feverishly on the rock floor before it was finally found. After that, each foot was placed with deliberation and there were no more frightening lurches.

At one point, the tunnel narrowed and they were crawling single file with water dripping down through cracks overhead onto their faces and necks. Sue's hands soon became skinned and bruised from feeling her way along the passage and she bit her lip hard to keep from whimpering as she leaned on the razor-sharp edges of rock. The only sound was the shuffle of their feet on the uneven surface and the intermittent rushes of small stones dislodged as they passed by. When that occurred, both froze like statues, instantly aware that a larger slide could mean eventual suffocation if they were pocketed under the earth.

Then abruptly the dank air became fresher even though the passage again had become so small that they were stooping and in single file.

Nick hesitated and put back a cautioning hand. "Stop a minute. I think we're almost there!"

Sue took a deep, shuddering breath. "I don't believe it."

"If I'm right ... there's only about twenty more feet."

"Then why don't we see some light?"

"Probably because of undergrowth blocking the entrance."

"Nick! What if this entrance is stopped up too!" she wailed.

"Nope," his breathing was almost as labored as hers. "Not with that much fresh air in our faces. Look! You can see the light filtering through the brush. ... Come on!"

Then he was scrabbling through the green growth and dragging her out in the clearing, where rain pelted down on their heads.

"Oh Nick!" The tears of joy on her cheeks were promptly washed away as they clung together.

Finally he pushed her back to arm's length saying, "Now, all we have to think about is getting back to the lodge before we drown." He chuckled as he focused on her face. "Lady . . . you look like an apprentice chimney sweep."

"It's no wonder ... I feel like one." She started to push her hair back and gasped as she noted the color of her palm. Her eyes flew up to Nick's smudged face and she bent over in helpless laughter. "At least we won't have to worry about the wild animals," she said finally, her shoulders still heaving with amusement. "One look at us and even a brown bear would turn tail."

"You're undoubtedly right, but I'd hate to put anything to the test after that damned shaft." He rubbed his forehead wearily, leaving a long, smeared streak above his eyebrows. "I hope this trail takes us where we want to go."

"It does. Unfortunately, we're on the far side of the mountain and we have to circle down and around the base. We'll be lucky to get back to the lodge by dark." She shivered as the rain penetrated her windbreaker.

"Let's get cracking." He gave her a worried look. "We were both a couple of chumps for not taking heavier jackets this morning."

"Don't you remember? The sun was shining when we started out." It was difficult to talk and keep up with his long strides. She looked up at him. "Besides, drowning doesn't seem so bad right now ... compared to other things. I don't think I'll even go down in a basement after this."

"Sure you will." His grasp tightened on her wrist. "The best thing for you to do is forget about that little episode. We made it."

"Thanks to you. I would have curled up and died."

"Stop talking like that." He determinedly changed the subject. "If you were a good Aleut woman, you'd have had a kamlaika ready for me when we came out into the rain."

"Do you eat it or wear it?"

"Pay attention and you'll find out. First ... you take the intestines of a seal or walrus," he began deliberately, "or if they aren't handy, you can use the skin off a whale's tongue...."

"I'm so glad ... I'd been wondering what to do with those old whales' tongues I had around the kitchen." She wiped her face with a sodden tissue she found in her pocket. "What next?"

"Sew it all together and you have a custom-made raincoat. Naturally you sew it with sinew, which will expand when it gets wet, thereby sealing the holes."

"Naturally. I suppose those friends of yours in Juneau told you all about Aleut raincoats."

"You don't have to live in Juneau to read Aleut history," he said noncommittally.

She nodded, deciding to abandon her probing for the moment. "The Indians had some good ideas, too. The Tlingits around here used to dry candlefish and use them as torches. They should have packaged them for exploring gold shafts."

"The very thing! When we get back to the lodge, we'll stock up on whale's tongues and dried candlefish."

"Idiot!"

"You don't agree?" He pushed aside some wet salal branches which were overhanging the trail.

"Nope. The first thing I'm going to do when I get back is to find a dry handkerchief so I can blow my nose properly. After that, I'll frame your cigarette lighter in the place of honor on the mantel." She had barely finished speaking when she sneezed explosively.

"Shake a leg, Sue." He put his arm over her shoulders as if trying to shield her from the now-driving rain. "If you aren't home pretty soon, the first thing I'll be doing is reserving a bed for you in the hospital pneumonia ward."

"If I go any faster, pneumonia will have to fight it out with a heart attack," she said, trying to catch her breath.

His arm slid down to encircle her waist. "Hang on to me."

"Hey! Things are getting better ... Big Chief Tired Wolf lettum squaw walk 'longside ... not three paces behind."

"Any more of that, young lady, and you'll be left considerably more than three paces behind."

"Threats too! If we get back before dark, I'll report you to the local chapter of Women's Liberation."

"I'll bet you would." He reached over and smacked her sharply on soggy slacks. "Now ... tell them I beat you, as well. Let's make it worthwhile."

"Brute!" Her grin was mischievous. "So that's why squaws always stayed three paces behind. *You* lead the way."

Despite Nick's determined pace on the trail, darkness was shrouding the trees around Wickitak when they finally struggled up the path and arrived at the front door of the lodge. The hike back would have been tiring in any circumstances; when combined with a steady downpour and those frightening hours in the tunnel, it was utterly exhausting. Sue felt the gates of Paradise couldn't have looked more welcome than that wide front door.

"Come on, Sue ... just a few more steps."

She leaned against the door jamb, watching him struggle with the heavy latch. "I didn't think I'd make the last fifty yards. Oh!" The exclamation burst out when Rock exploded into their midst, yelping and whining in ecstasy

"Down, boy!" Nick commanded finally. "Did you think you'd been abandoned forever?"

"Poor Rocko," Sue crooned as she sank onto the bottom step of the stairs and hugged the shaggy brown head to her breast. "He can't stand being alone."

The Airedale's crook of a tail beat a tattoo against the newel post while his tongue assured her that the apology was accepted.

"Poor Rocko nothing," Nick said, pulling her to her feet. "He's completely recovered now that you're home again."

"Ummm ... I hope so. He's probably starving."

"Aren't we all—but first things first." He gave her a severe look. "I'm prescribing a hot bath for you. Can you manage the stairs or shall I carry you?"

"I'm fine," she insisted although her feet felt like two cold bars of lead as she placed them on the steps. "Do you suppose Marie left something in the refrigerator?"

"There's bound to be food somewhere." He put an unobtrusive arm around her waist when she sagged with weariness at the top of the stairs. "Get in your room," he said, opening the door. "Shed those wet clothes while I run your bath. And for lord's sake, find a flannel nightgown to wear afterwards instead of something drafty. Did your uncle leave a wool robe in his closet?"

"It's miles too big," she protested.

"So much the better. You can wrap it around twice. Move, woman!" he growled as she hesitated. "If you're worried about modesty, I'll go out the hall door after I've started running your bath water."

He strode into the bathroom and the noise of water gushing from the taps was the next welcome sound. Rock trotted happily behind him to investigate the happenings.

"Rock ... get out of there!" Nick yelled suddenly. "Damnation!"

"What's the matter?" she called in alarm.

"Nothing much." He sounded resigned. "I should have asked what you wanted in the bath besides some crumbs of cheese-flavored dog biscuit. They were on his whiskers."

Her shoulders shook with laughter as she peeled away a sodden shirt. "Never mind. See if there's any cheese-flavored bubble bath in the cabinet. Otherwise, there's a pine scent strong enough to blanket anything."

There was a lengthy pause and then, "Okay, it's all ready. If I don't hear this door close in two minutes, I'll come back and dump you in the water myself."

"You wouldn't dare!" Her fingers became thumbs as she unzipped her slacks.

"I mean it."

"So do I...." She went over to the bureau and pawed frantically through a drawer for a flannel gown. "I'll be there in about thirty seconds."

"Okay. Don't fall asleep."

"I haven't drowned in a bathtub yet," she called indignantly.

He was unimpressed. "Afterwards, get right to bed. I'll bring your supper up."

"You needn't spoil me to that extent...." The slam of the hall door was the only answer she received. She peered around the corner of the bathroom door and then closed it carefully behind her as she padded into the empty room, sniffing the steamy air happily. A shiver coursed her body as she put her nightgown on the hamper. It would be wonderful to be warm again. When she submerged in the fragrant frothy water, it was the most glorious sensation imaginable. She stretched out, blissfully letting her head rest against the end of the tub, and closed her eyes.

The minutes slipped by as she relaxed until she heard steps in the hall. She sat up quickly and then slid back under the bubbles just as quickly when a rap came on the bathroom door.

"Wha ... what is it?" She had to clear her throat to get the words out.

"Just checking to see if you were still alive in there."

She stood up and reached for a towel. "If that's a hint—I'm getting out right now."

"Good. I put a couple of hot-water bottles in your bed and draped that wool dressing gown of your uncle's over the foot of it."

She paused in her brisk toweling. "Are you sure all this is necessary?"

"I wouldn't be doing it otherwise," came the terse reply. "Do as you're told ... I'll bring you something to eat in a few minutes." His footsteps faded down the hall.

She had followed his instructions to the letter by the time he reappeared half an hour later. Fortunately, the robe was a shade of green which provided an attractive foil for her auburn hair. Even more important, she had discovered, its wide lapels hid the high-necked horror of her white flannel nightgown. That garment's utilitarian lines were more suited to the plague ward than anywhere else. At least, no one could accuse her of trying to vamp Nicholas in it; its severe design would send any red-blooded man fleeing in the opposite direction.

Nick's footsteps had sounded on the stairs while she was debating the merits of lipstick. She applied a pale one in two hurried swipes and then made a leap into the big mahogany bed as a thud came against the bottom of the hall door.

"Are you receiving?" he called.

"Just barely ... come in." She watched him

struggle with the doorknob and try to balance a large oval tray at the same time. "I'll help you...." She started to push back the covers.

"Get back there...." His deep voice halted her abruptly. "Is it all right to put anything on this?" He hovered beside the round piecrust lamp table near the head of the bed.

"Of course." She cleared a paperback book out of the way and watched him deposit the laden tray. "Ummm ... smells like soup in the mugs. What's under the covered dish?"

"Melted cheese sandwiches. There's tea in the thermos, if you want it."

"It sounds wonderful!" She looked up at him. "You are going to eat with me, aren't you?"

"If I'm invited." His slow grin appeared. "Rock will be up shortly. He's consuming a dinosaur bone in the kitchen at the moment."

She nodded. "Pull up that chair and make yourself comfortable—you must be exhausted after all your activity. I checked with Cal on the radio a few minutes ago." She sorted the napkins and then reached for a mug of steaming soup. "There didn't seem to be any need to tell him about our trouble this afternoon."

"I'm all for that." He sank down in an upholstered chair and swallowed his own soup. His eyes narrowed as they took in her flushed cheeks. "What's the matter? Did your gentleman friend read you a lecture?"

"How did you know?" She grimaced in acknowledgment of his amused look. "Cal has exaggerated ideas of propriety."

"I take it he wasn't keen on our being alone here for the night."

"That's about it," she admitted. "It was certainly a lot of fuss about nothing; Marie will be back tomorrow on the mail boat." Her expression lightened as Rock came into the room carrying a large, denuded bone. "Besides ... we have a chaperon."

"A formidable adversary," he murmured.

"You mean Rock, of course?"

"Of course."

Her eyes met his levelly. "He can be."

"I'm sure of that." The words were casual. "I hope you were able to convince your ... friend ... that all was strictly platonic."

"My ... friend ..." she mimicked him expertly, "was told in no uncertain terms."

"Good."

"He was happier when I told him I'd go down to Juneau this weekend for certain."

"What does that involve?"

"Dinner and dancing usually. I stay in a room at the hotel...." She intercepted a calculating glance and added deliberately, "A single room at the hotel. Cal lives in an apartment over his business."

"You don't have to explain."

"I wouldn't want ... anyone ... to get a

mistaken impression." Her knuckles were as white as the sheet she was clutching. She went on carefully. "I hope you don't mind being abandoned here. Cal said there was a possibility that Florence and her party might stay in town for the weekend as well."

He deposited his mug on the tray and passed the sandwiches before sitting back down. "That's the best news yet. Tell me . . ." he took a bite and chewed it thoughtfully, "has Marie worked for your uncle long?"

His abrupt change of subject made her lean forward. "She and Joe have been here about ten years." She frowned down at the sandwich in her hand and then looked over at him. "Why? What's wrong?"

He shook his head irritably. "Nothing. At least, nothing worth bothering about. When I went in my room to take a shower, I noticed that some of my belongings had been shifted around. It wasn't as if they'd been stirred with a spoon . . . just moved."

"Was anything missing?"

"Not that I could see." He dusted his hands on a paper napkin and rose to pour the tea. "Probably Marie was straightening things."

"Probably. It needn't have been Marie, you know. All three of the others were still in their rooms after you went out this morning."

His eyebrows drew into a straight line. "I hadn't thought of that."

"You didn't go back to your room after breakfast, did you?"

"No ... but why in the deuce should any of them be interested in the contents of my bureau drawers?"

She shrugged. "I can't imagine ... but what do we really know about any of them?"

"Hardly enough to make it interesting. Florence makes noises about being a retired schoolteacher ..."

"... who specializes in woodcarving and the history of gold mines." She chewed on her lower lip. "I've seen her carving and it's terrible. That doesn't prove anything except that she probably wasn't an art teacher. As for the interest in gold mines ..."

"That doesn't mean a thing. Nine out of ten women would be intensely interested in anything to do with gold. And if Florence is a retired teacher, the historical angle might have more than usual appeal."

"So that brings us to Leo."

He stared absently into his tea. "You can wash him out, too."

"After an entire day on the boat?" Her voice rose incredulously.

"Believe me, he was not exchanging confidences over the baiting of his hook. There were a few remarks dropped about 'various business enterprises' but nothing specific." He grinned unexpectedly. "On the other hand, if there's any information needed about catching anything from minnows to killer whales, Leo will be happy to supply it."

"He sounds like one of those seafood restaurants that advertises 'If it swims—we have it' at the top of the menu."

"In Leo's case, 'If it swims—he's caught it.'" His grin lingered. "That's probably why he doesn't show much interest in Monica—she doesn't have fins."

"They're the only things she's missing."

"There are a few others," he assured her.

"Umm, I don't know about that."

"Don't lose any sleep over it." He took a swallow of tea. "Does it strike you that Monica acts different from most secretaries?"

Her laughter bubbled out. "That's an understatement! Monica's made up of mysteries. For one thing, that wardrobe of hers wasn't purchased on a secretary's salary. For another, unless Leo is nursing a hidden passion, he isn't the one who buys those elegant clothes for her."

"You're right on one point; Leo's only passion is hooking a forty-pound salmon. I'd put money on that!"

"So there you are. Monica isn't forthcoming with funds of information, either. At least," she said pointedly, "not to me."

He didn't rise to the bait. "Wasn't there any tip-off in their reservation correspondence?"

"Nope. Apparently Uncle Tim confirmed their reservation verbally before he left to go abroad."

"They're safe in saying that. Even if you checked by sending an aerogramme to the Maputo Game Reserve, it would take time."

"So . . . what do you suggest we do?"

He let out a thoughtful sigh. "There's nothing to do except wait and see."

"If you want to put any valuables away, there's a safe in the study."

"Aside from a few traveler's checks, my tangible assets could be left on the front porch," he said cheerfully. "Don't worry. There's undoubtedly a logical explanation for the whole thing and we'll find out in time. Meanwhile, let's forget it." He stood up. "I'll take the dishes away if you're finished."

She swallowed her tea hastily and handed over the cup and saucer. "Yes, sir—right away, sir—and thank you, sir."

"You can cut that out, too." He pushed the dishes in a neat pile and lifted the tray. "I suggest that you turn out the lamp and go right to sleep."

"All right." She smiled as he stepped carefully over Rock. "Nick?"

He paused by the door and glanced back over his shoulder. As his eyes took in the attractive picture she made, a slight uneasiness spread over his expression. The lamplight picked up coppery bits in her soft hair and blue eyes looked darker than ever when framed by faint shadows of weariness. "What's the matter?" His voice was tense. "Did I forget something?"

"No ... I wanted to say thank you," she said simply.

He started to make an offhand gesture and then found he was still clutching the tray. "Forget it."

"That isn't easy. I didn't mean that you had to take the job literally when I hired you."

His forehead wrinkled until fleeting realization softened his features. "Caretaker, you mean?" The crooked grin flickered. "I didn't know about the side benefits or I would have been up here weeks before."

The silence held until Rock moved his bone closer to Sue's bed and she leaned over automatically to fend him off.

"I'll be on my way." Nick was back to his usual brisk self. "Hope you don't have any bad effects from the afternoon."

She strove to retrieve that golden moment. "Bad effects? You mean nightmares from 'ghoulies and ghosties and things that go bump in the night'? I haven't been warned away from those since I was a little girl."

He wasn't tempted by her obvious diversion. "They're some of the hazards but not exactly the ones I meant. If I were you, I'd do my best to scrub out the whole day. There was nothing about it worth remembering. Good night."

This time the door closed firmly behind him.

Sue fell back against the pillows, her face as drained of emotion as his. What on earth had brought on that cutting remark? There wasn't anything in a simple "thank you" to make him veer off like a startled hare. It wasn't as if she had expected anything other than a pleasant acknowledgment in return.

Or had she?

She made a major project out of shaking her pillows before turning off the light. If she was distraught, it was because she was tired. The involuntary shiver that coursed her body was the aftermath of her chill—nothing more.

Rock corkscrewed into the rug by her side and sighed wearily. She put down a hand and absently scratched behind his ears. There was no point in counting sheep, she decided. The thing to think about was the weekend full of fun and relaxation with Cal in Juneau.

Concentrate on that—and forget the tall, solemn man who made her feel as welcome as a Tax Due notice from Internal Revenue. Forget him at the same time she was forgetting the black hole of an abandoned mining shaft. She flounced restlessly on the mattress, wishing she could relax her painful thoughts as easily as her aching muscles. Determinedly, she closed her eyes and willed sleep to come.

It was the middle of the night when she was shaken abruptly into wakefulness. She blinked in confusion as she focused on Nick's tall figure, which bent over her in concern. Light from the hallway revealed his rumpled hair and the hastily belted robe thrown on over his pajamas.

As he saw her startled glance, he drew back and dropped her wrists.

"Don't look like that!" His voice was rough. "You screamed and scared the sweet hell out of me. That's why I barged in here."

Wonderingly she became conscious of wet cheeks and put up a hand to dry them. "I'm sorry . . . it was a nightmare." She took a deep, hiccuping breath as she tried to recall. "There was something about a black pit—I couldn't get out."

"I thought you were having a bad dream when I came stumbling to the rescue and found you sobbing in your sleep. I almost landed head-first in your bed when I fell over your damned dog."

She struggled up on an elbow. "Where is he?"

He jerked his head toward the open door. "Out in the hall recovering from his own nervous breakdown. I think he would have taken my leg off at the knee if you'd screamed once more."

It was hard to be dignified when she must look like an illustration for a horror story, but Sue made the effort. She disregarded her overwhelming inclination to say "Please Nick—let me borrow your shoulder for just five minutes and I won't bother you any more tonight." The memory of his brusque leave-taking earlier in the evening was still too vivid to allow any liberties. Even the uncertain look he was giving her now—as if he were truly worried about how she felt—couldn't erase it.

Resolutely she pulled the sheet up over her shoulder as if she were closing a curtain on the entire scene. "Do you suppose we could cut this short," she managed casually. "I'm sorry about this overtime effort, Nick. I'll have to rescue you one of these days."

Her airy tones caused him to stiffen. "Forget it," he said, finally. "You don't need any Brownie points." He turned on his heel and strode out to the hall.

A minute later, she heard his bedroom door slam behind him.

Rock chose that moment to pad back into the room and collapse by her bed.

"Thanks a lot for helping," she told him bitterly. "Where were you when I needed you?"

He arranged his chin on her bedroom slippers and bestowed one reproachful look before deliberately closing his eyes. Obviously, as far as he was concerned, any further conversation was going to be strictly one-sided.

Sue's bad dream didn't reappear for the rest of the night.

Probably because she couldn't manage to close her eyes long enough to have made it worthwhile.

Chapter Six

The red and silver wings of Cal's Cessna 180 flashed in the crisp sunshine Friday afternoon when he banked for a landing on Juneau's Gastineau channel.

"How does the old town look, Susie?" He was giving all his attention to the water below, looking out for floating logs or debris which could spell tragedy for the pontoons of a small floatplane.

She forced herself to concentrate on the panorama of Alaska's capital built on the steep coastal hills with their thin fiordlike fingers. The big car ferry which was part of the state's famed maritime highway was pulling away from its city pier. It would steam south on its solid, plodding way until hitting the open ocean waters of Queen Charlotte Sound, when it would begin to writhe like a tortured, live thing over those huge swells. In a boat harbor to the north, the jig poles of trolling craft looked like white snags of dead trees against the backdrop of forested hills. Out in the channel, a small sailboat curtsied lazily in the wake of a speeding power cruiser while farther uptown, cars were almost at a standstill on the one-way street near the tall federal building.

Sue braced her hand against the side of the plane and sat upright. "Juneau's beginning to look like a big city, Cal. You'd better head north and get away from all this civilization."

"Nope . . . this is the way I've learned to like it." Easily, deftly he set the plane down on the channel water and started taxiing toward a long float labeled Northland. "The more people down here in the southeast part of the state—the more business for me. The more business—the more money I make and the more times I can take my favorite redhead out to dinner." He maneuvered alongside a ramp where one of his men was waiting to secure the plane. "What time do you want to eat tonight?"

She waited for him to cut the engine before unbuckling her seat belt and scrambling behind him out onto the dock. "Not until I can change out of these slacks into something more presentable." She shook back her hair and watched him reach up into the plane for her small overnight case.

"Okay . . . if that won't take too long." He walked beside her up the inclined ramp to his sparsely furnished but busy headquarters. "I'm hoping to get off early."

Several men turned to smile at Sue as she and Cal threaded their way through the piles of freight in the warehouse area.

"There'll be a taxi along in a minute, Miss Strathern," a secretary called from behind a counter. "I telephoned when I saw you touch down."

"Thanks very much." Sue gave her a friendly wave and followed Cal out the wide door onto the sidewalk.

A taxi was just pulling up at the curb.

"How's that for service?" Cal reached over to open the front door for her and casually slung her case onto the back seat. His tall frame bent almost double as he directed the driver to take her to Juneau's newest hotel on busy Franklin Street.

"Thanks Cal," she murmured gratefully as she got in the cab. "I'll be in my room from six on. Give me a call when you know what your schedule is going to be."

The rest of the afternoon passed quickly with a short session at the hairdresser's and a shopping spree at the hotel's boutique. When Cal telephoned from the lobby, she was arrayed in her newest purchases and fully determined to make the most of her evening out.

Any diversion would be welcome after the last two days at the lodge, she decided, as she poked the elevator button. Cal needn't have worried about propriety; Nick's coldly formal behavior toward her would have been approved of by a puritan elder. Marie, who had returned on the mail boat, provided a go-between when dialogue was absolutely necessary. The conversational gambits ranged from

"Please pass the salt" to a fascinating discussion on how long the low-pressure area would linger over the mountains. They remained punctiliously polite to each other, although after one such exchange Sue caught a gleam of humor in his eyes.

Cal greeted her with a low whistle of admiration when she stepped out of the elevator. He held her at arm's length to carefully inspect her new outfit, a flaring green print tunic and black crepe dinner pants.

"Say ... I like it! What did they call those ladies of the harems?"

"I think you mean a houri," she said, coloring slightly. "But their outfits were transparent and were worn for quite a different purpose."

"Damn ... wouldn't you know!" He sighed theatrically and then grinned at her expression. "C'mon—we can discuss those different purposes over a drink before dinner." Her hand was tucked under his elbow and she was towed along into a doorway opening off the lobby.

They were ushered to a table in the corner of a dimly lit dining room where the decor emphasized a turn-of-the-century motif in keeping with Alaskan history. Russian influence especially was evident in the intricately designed lighting fixtures and the heavy brass samovar displayed on a mammoth buffet.

Cal waited until their order was taken and

the drinks delivered to their table before he went back to their conversation. "When I see you in an outfit like that, honey, I wonder why I don't spend all my time sitting on your doorstep."

"You almost commute as it is." She raised her glass in a silent toast. "Thanks for taking Marie down the other day, by the way. She's going to fetch Joe out of the hospital the first of the week."

"I could come and get her...."

"She'll travel with Captain Fergus. You won't have a business at all if you continue to spoil us."

He leaned across the table and covered her hand with his. "You should know by now that I'd like to do it on a full-time basis."

Sue let her hand remain motionless for a minute and then turned it over to grasp his. "Cal dear—don't talk like that. There's no future in it."

"But why?"

She gently slipped her hand away and sat back. "A pair of redheads and you talk about a merger!" Her tone was whimsical. "You know what happens when people of our temperament get together. Sparks fly."

He remained hunched over the table, his rangy physique collecting an admiring glance from a passing waitress. "Is that bad? You get a bonfire from sparks too."

She shook her head regretfully.

"Think about it for a while," he insisted. "I'll bet I could change your mind."

"There's an expression for that—something about 'one to kiss and one to turn the cheek.' Frankly, it sounds awful to me." She gave him a level look. "And you're too much of a man to put up with that for long."

He leaned back and reached for his drink. "I'm not going to give up," he insisted stubbornly.

"I wish you would. Don't you see, Cal—there shouldn't be anything one-sided about falling in love. It isn't fair for one person to do all the hoping and yearning...." her words trailed off as she noted his questioning look. "Besides, you're much too restless to think of settling down right now. You fell in love with a floatplane five years ago and there isn't a woman alive who could compete." She smiled slightly. "Not that a few haven't tried."

"If you're going to rake over old coals...."

"Heavens no. Let's change the subject ... this is supposed to be a party."

His answering grin didn't quite reach his eyes. "All right, Susie. Don't look so desperate. We'll consider the subject scrubbed for tonight." His finger traced a design down the side of his icy glass as he changed the topic. "Tim left you with a handful at Wickitak, didn't he?"

"When Joe was hurt, it was quite a thrash, but things are under control now." She took a sip of her drink. "I'm glad you sold my trio on that trip to Glacier Bay—that's how I could get away this weekend."

"They're back here in Juneau, you know."

"Oh?" She gave him a surprised glance. "I knew they were returning to the lodge Sunday morning, but I hadn't realized they were in town yet."

He nodded. "I flew them in early this morning. Leo had some business to handle."

"How did Monica survive the icebergs?"

"Where that woman is—ice isn't." He poked at the ice cube in his drink. "By the time she goes home, half the glaciers in the state will be receding."

"I didn't know she'd made such an impression. No . . . that isn't true. That darned woman could bring an Egyptian mummy to life."

"She was practicing on me," he admitted complacently.

"Of course . . . keeping a hand in."

"If you mean literally—then no."

"I refuse to pursue that subject either."

"You don't have to," he said abruptly as he started getting to his feet. "She's coming this way."

"You mean Monica? Oh no!" Her dismayed whisper scarcely reached across the table.

"I mean the whole caboodle." He was

watching the three of them as they left the bar and made their way through the tables. "Good evening," he said jovially as they came up. "Apparently we all had the same idea for a night out." Only someone who knew him well could have detected the undertone of annoyance in his voice.

"There's not much choice in this town," Monica said flatly. "Hello, Sue . . . did the open spaces get you down or did you have a fight with Nick?"

"No fights." Sue crossed her fingers in her lap and wished for the umpteenth time the other wasn't so perceptive. She turned to Florence. "Will you join us?"

"No thank you, dear." The older woman rested her hand lightly on the back of Sue's chair. "I've had such an exhausting day that I'm going up to my room and laze around." She looked inquiringly at her nephew. "What about you, Leo?"

He shrugged. "Might as well stay down here for dinner as hibernate in a hotel room. Monica?"

That young woman answered by sliding gracefully into the extra chair a waiter was obligingly holding at the table. "I'll stay here; the bright lights might be a little dim, but it's better than nothing."

"Thanks," Cal said sardonically.

"Sweetie . . . forgive me." Her voice reflected

an immediate change of mood. "I didn't mean anything personal. It's wonderful to see you—and Sue, of course—after a steady diet of scenery."

"I meant to ask how you'd enjoyed your trip," Sue said to Florence.

"It was lovely . . . Leo took loads of pictures. Did you know that there was ice three thousand feet thick over that entire area just two hundred fifty years ago?" Florence's expression was rapt. "This afternoon, we went out to see the Mendenhall glacier. You wouldn't believe that ice could be so blue!"

"They've seen it, Flo." Leo was obviously embarrassed by her ecstatic tone. He hovered uncertainly by an empty chair. "You don't mind if Monica and I desert you?"

"Of course not, dear boy." She patted his arm in motherly fashion. "You young people have a good time."

"What about your dinner?" he asked.

"I'll call room service. Frankly, I can't wait to change into something comfortable and spend the evening watching television." Her eyes crinkled with amusement. "There'll be a time when you feel that way, too—so enjoy yourselves now." She bestowed a final beam on them and tripped away.

"I hope you're ready to eat," Monica said, reaching for a menu. "Frankly, I'm starving."

Sue intercepted the rueful glance Cal sent

across to her and nodded in return. Evidently their restful evening out had disappeared. She took the menu the waiter was offering. "We'll order now if you like."

Leo was painstakingly checking the list of entrees. "I hope they have something that's on my diet," he said. "I've missed Marie's cooking these last two days."

"She'll be flattered to hear that," Sue murmured politely.

"Fortunately, I always travel well prepared for emergencies," he confided, happy to find a kindred soul. "If you have any trouble with your stomach, Sue—give me a call. Day or night, it makes no difference." He peered solemnly at her over the top of the menu. "A person can't be too careful, you know."

Sue hid behind the wine list until she could manage a straight face. A quick peek to see if Cal had heard revealed his head huddled close to Monica's as they laughed over something the dark-haired woman had just said. Evidently Leo's secretary had assessed the two men and calmly decided to switch escorts. Her rating gave a healthy pilot priority over her employer's gastric distress.

Sue fought down a strong impulse to leave the table and just disappear.

It was harder to fight down her desire to be back at Wickitak—a feeling that had persistently haunted her ever since she had left the lodge. The cold misery of it had hovered about her all day and now it was making a travesty of her holiday. This was more than an evening going awry; it was as if her very existence had turned from its pleasant, normal course and become something to endure. Endure was certainly the right word, she decided with a flicker of humor, as Leo's monologue continued in her ear.

"Do scallops ever give you indigestion?" he was asking.

"Not generally," she said after considering the question, "but the way I'm feeling tonight—there's a good possibility."

Even by the next morning, things had not improved appreciably.

The first blow came when Cal phoned to say he would be tied up all day with a sudden charter. "It's the owner of one of the trollers," he told her gloomily. "He wants me to fly him down to Ketchikan to see a man about some fish ... ten thousand pounds of them, I guess. I'm afraid it'll take up most of the day."

"Don't worry about it," she tried to reassure him. "You can't afford to alienate any customers."

"Just so I don't alienate you. I *did* invite you down for the weekend and it hasn't been much so far. Last night was sure a drag."

She refrained from mentioning that he

hadn't appeared to suffer throughout the evening.

The evasion evidently penetrated because his tone became subdued. "I'm sorry you were stuck with Leo so long last night."

"Forget it. We found we had a lot in common —one stomach, one digestive tract, and we're both mad for the same kind of cough drop."

The nuances in her cheerful words escaped him. "That's good," he said with relief. "I was afraid you might be a little annoyed this morning."

"Heavens no. Take off on your charter and concentrate on your fisherman," she said, realizing suddenly that she would have hung up long ago if she were in love with him. "Be sure and save enough time tomorrow to get us back to the lodge, though. I promised Marie without fail."

"No problems, sweetie. Let's have a late breakfast. Sunday is the one day I can goof off."

"We'll see. Let us know what time you want to take off."

"Right. Have a good day." He rang off.

"Have a good day indeed!" she said to herself, looking around the austere hotel room. Obviously, those four walls wouldn't suffice for long. It was a pity she wasn't like Florence, content to pull on her furry slippers and spend the day watching television.

She kicked irritably at a piece of lint on the

rug and then, realizing the futility of such a gesture, reached down and put it in the wastebasket. There was a time to mope and a time not to mope. Ten o'clock on a sunny Saturday forenoon in Juneau was not the time. It *was* the time for looking in the shops, having lunch in a good restaurant, and staying far, far away from the other inhabitants of Wickitak Lodge.

A walk along the waterfront should be safe later in the day; Florence would be napping in her room, Monica wouldn't stir out on foot, and Leo had mentioned a forthcoming doctor's appointment.

She found herself smiling in anticipation as she pulled on an amethyst knit suit with a boxy jacket and pleated skirt. She slipped a silk kerchief of a deeper shade into her purse in case the weather changed quickly. A glance in the mirror confirmed that she was presentable for the street. Really a little more than presentable, she decided judiciously, and blithely went out the door.

The rest of the day passed pleasantly as she stuck to her plans and successfully avoided the rest of her party. Window shopping was leisurely and lunch beyond criticism. Leo's fears for her digestion were happily groundless, she discovered. All she needed was a brisk walk in the clear air afterwards.

Her visit to the city museum's new exhibit of Indian artifacts brought Leo back to mind briefly. As she looked at magical potions of the shaman or tribal medicine man, it occurred to her that Leo had at least one medical source still untapped.

She had completed her tour of the displays and was on her way out when Nick's tall figure in front of a nearby glass exhibit case stopped her in her tracks.

He turned around while she was wondering whether to vanish or tap him on the shoulder. "Well," he said slowly, "this is a surprise. I didn't think you'd be wandering around here by yourself."

"I often spend some time here when I'm in town," she said after a brief glance at his amused features. "I thought I might be able to use some of the Indian lore in an article for the magazine. After all, they had handy household hints long before Heloise."

"I noticed." He adopted the pontifical tone of a television announcer. "If you get a hole in your canoe ... don't throw it away and buy a new one ..."

"Just chew hard on globules of resin and soften them for a patch," she finished for him. "Of course, if you have time, it's better to use the spruce-gum boiling method. While you're waiting, an afternoon snack of dried salmon and berries dunked in eulachon oil makes the hours pass quickly. If you'd like the recipe for this and other Alaskan treats. . . ."

"Send a brown bear, three caribou, and a Dall sheep to your local station, along with a stamped, self-addressed envelope," he concluded, chuckling. "I'll know better than to try and impress you with any Indian history from now on. It's either find my own museum or give up." He bestowed a quizzical look. "If you can remember things like that, why do you draw a blank on how much water to put in dehydrated eggs?"

"I thought we'd agreed to forget that." There was absolutely no squelching of the man, Sue decided. She addressed a compass point above and beyond those broad shoulders. "I didn't expect to find you wandering around Juneau," she said, choosing an offensive tack for a change.

"Even caretakers get a day off."

"You know that's not what I meant. Why didn't you fly down yesterday with us?"

"I decided at the last minute to get a couple of spare parts for that generator motor. Besides, if you'll remember—we weren't on the most cordial terms when you left."

"Whose fault was that?" She moved aside to let a party of school children get through the hall.

"Come on," he took her arm impatiently and pushed her out onto the front steps of the building, "let's finish our discussion where there's more room."

She pulled loose to confront him. "We're practically finished. The only things we talk about are the weather and whether you'd like a cup of coffee."

He glanced up at the sky. "It looks like rain and I don't want any coffee, thanks."

"There you are then...." She fought down a feeling of melancholy and started to pull on her gloves. "We've run the conversational gamut."

"You didn't let me finish." He signaled for a cruising cab and opened the door as it pulled up to the curb. "I was going to say that at this time of the afternoon, I'd rather have a drink—with you. Get in."

Being a sensible woman, Sue got in. "Let's not go to the hotel bar," she said evenly, "unless you want to take a chance on meeting Leo and Monica."

He nodded agreeably. "There's a place next door to it. We'll go there."

In a short time, they were comfortably ensconced in a quiet cocktail lounge and surveying each other across a small table.

While they were waiting for their drinks to arrive, he said "Rocko sent his best."

"I'm surprised at that," she admitted. "He's been sulking ever since I startled him with that nightmare. I'm taking back a new rubber bone to make amends."

"Had any more of those lately? Nightmares . . . I mean."

She made a wry grimace as she picked up her glass of sherry. "Awake or sleeping?"

"That's a loaded question." He tried to analyze her expression. "Do I get an explanation or should I let it ride?"

"There wasn't any Freudian symbolism behind it. I guess I was thinking about the deadly time I had last night."

"Did something go wrong on your date with Cal?"

"It turned out to be Monica's date with Cal," she corrected ironically. "Leo and I shared honors at the other side of the table."

Nick's look was hard to interpret. "There'll be other dates. I'd offer to waylay Monica tonight, but I've made other plans. . . ."

"That isn't necessary—as far as I'm concerned, I mean." Her words tumbled out in explanation. "For one thing, I don't have a date with Cal tonight."

"Good lord, you can't mean he's taking Monica seriously?"

"Cal is never serious for long about any woman," she said, amending the truth slightly but determined that Nick shouldn't be misled again. "He's busy all day on a charter. I don't expect to see him until we fly home tomorrow."

"I see." His voice was thoughtful. "It's too bad we didn't meet sooner."

"Yes, isn't it." The conventional answer gave no indication of the depth of her feeling. As he made no reply, she went on brightly, "Did you come on the mail boat with Captain Fergus?"

He nodded absently. "We got in about noon."

"Pleasant trip?"

"Very quiet most of the time." That slow grin appeared. "Not all of the time though."

"What do you mean?"

"The captain's a frustrated musician. He and that deckhand of his spent a good part of the trip showing off on their harmonicas."

"I didn't know they were so talented."

"They get along pretty well. At one point, they were even trying some harmony." He chuckled. "The only trouble came when the captain was playing the 'Skye Boat Song' and his young friend was on the second chorus of 'Suwanee River.'"

"You should have helped out."

"I did. I was steering the boat and humming off-key."

She burst out laughing. "I wish I'd been there."

"I wish you had, too. We could have used a soprano. Are you another budding musician?"

"Heavens no—I just like to listen. One of these days my mind is going to rust away from inactivity."

"I refuse to believe that." He rotated the ice

in his glass. "Obviously, your talents run in other directions."

"If you mention trail breakfasts or dehydrated eggs again, I might forget I'm a lady."

"Pax. I promise to ignore the subjects."

She pushed back her cuff and looked at her watch. "It's time I was going. . . ."

"Look," he cut in abruptly, "if you don't have other plans—will you have dinner with me tonight?"

"You don't have to be polite. You said a few minutes ago that you had other plans."

"I have to meet someone and you should fit in very well," he told her. "Monica wouldn't."

"Are you sure?"

"Take my word for it. You should know by now that I don't generally play games."

"I don't know a darned thing," she countered rebelliously. "Not even why we're suddenly speaking after two days in that frosty atmosphere. And that was your fault," she added with conviction.

"Just at the beginning. Look—let's not go over it right now. Take my word for it that I had a good reason."

"Well . . . all right." She kept her gaze on the table top. "We'll consider it ancient history and proceed from there."

There was no use volunteering the information that, for some strange reason, he could get his way on most anything he wanted to ask. She darted a quick look at him from under lowered lashes, observing the tanned skin stretched over sharp cheekbones and the strong line of his jaw. There was decision in his manner even as he signaled a waiter and asked for a menu. Nick was evidently one of those fortunate individuals who expected no quarter from life's problems and demanded none, a man's man who could succeed in making any woman forget her resolutions when she was around him.

"Is that all right with you?"

She heard his voice but the words didn't register until she saw him glancing at her quizzically. "I beg your pardon?"

"I was asking if you minded eating here. It only runs to sandwiches but at least we won't be interrupted."

"Oh yes . . . please. A sandwich will be fine."

He grinned. "You can't complain that I dazzle a woman with heavy spending—an afternoon at the museum and a roast beef sandwich for dinner."

"Don't suggest that we go Dutch," she threatened. "After listening to Leo last night, I was about to dispense with the male sex completely."

"As bad as that, eh? You'd better take a little time before you make that decision."

"I intend to." Her eyes glinted mischievously. "Aren't you going to take up the cudgels and defend the cause of masculinity?"

"Hell no. I think it's a fine idea if you dislike most men." There was only a shade of emphasis laid on his last two words but it was there. He continued to survey the menu casually. "We can improve on this by having dessert with a friend of mine. She always has something on hand."

"She?"

"She," he said definitely. "A very old friend. You'll like her."

Her opposition evaporated in the warmth of his gaze. Greatly to her astonishment she heard her own voice murmuring demurely, "I'm sure I will, Nick."

And she did.

From the minute the taxi deposited them in front of an old-fashioned house on one of Juneau's hillsides and she caught a glimpse of the tiny, gray-haired woman waiting to greet them.

Nick bent down to kiss his hostess on the cheek before saying, "I brought a friend of mine along, Lennie. May I present Sue Strathern. Sue—this is Lennie Brock, who's known me so long that she can cut me down to size without half-trying."

Sue smiled warmly. "How do you do, Mrs. Brock. I've been waiting to meet someone who could handle Nick like that."

"I'm happy to know you, dear." The older

woman took Sue's outstretched hand in a gentle clasp. "I'll tell you the secrets of my success with this rascal later—but now let's get in out of the wind. I have a fireplace fire to keep us company in the living room."

She led the way through a small foyer, where Nick paused to hang his trench coat on a curved oak hall tree before following into the high-ceilinged living room. A bright blaze crackled in the brick fireplace near the end of it.

Lennie motioned toward the davenport in front of the fireplace. "Sit down, my dears. Have you eaten?"

"Just finished, Lennie," Nick said.

"Can't you manage some pie?" Her expression was woebegone.

Sue broke out laughing. "We certainly could. Nick promised faithfully that you'd offer dessert."

"Well, I should hope so. I'll get it right away."

"Can I help?"

"No thank you, child. All I have to do is pour the coffee and carry in the tray."

"Carrying in trays is my specialty," Nick told Sue. "Sit down and get warm. We'll be back in two shakes."

She watched him put an affectionate arm around the other's shoulders and disappear with her toward the kitchen.

Before sitting down in front of the fire, Sue walked over to gaze through the long windows overlooking the town and harbor. Multicolored lights and neon signs on the buildings far below put a festive air on the city's early darkness. In the harbor area, the afterdeck of a Canadian cruise ship was outlined in white lights while out on the water, the red and green running lights of smaller vessels moved steadily along. A sudden gust of wind rattled the window glass and she shivered involuntarily. September weather always seemed poised on the brink—only needing a nudge to change from fall's crispness to winter's icy breaths.

She moved back to the couch and sat staring into the fire.

At least she wouldn't have to worry about Alaskan weather. By the time winter really flexed its muscles, she'd be buried in a steam-heated Manhattan skyscraper. Her head went back to rest on the cushion. Buried was certainly the proper word, she decided. The last week had made her realize that any glamourous aspects of her job had slipped into the routine category. She chewed on her lower lip and decided to face a few facts: fact number one—part of that new-found dislike for Manhattan's landscape might be due to the knowledge that Nicholas Dunbar wasn't in it; fact number two—nor was he apt to be. Their conversation over sandwiches and coffee had revealed that cities held little fascination for him.

"Fortunately, I haven't had to spend much time in them," he had said. "I think your Uncle Tim has the right idea."

"You should ask him if he wants an assistant manager at Wickitak."

"It's the best offer I've had today," he assured her solemnly, "I'll think it over." Beyond that, he had refused to be drawn.

Sue snuggled deeper into the comfortable davenport and relaxed. At least she might as well stop fussing and enjoy Nick's company while she could.

"Did you think we were taking forever?" Lennie bustled back into the room carrying a silver coffeepot and Nick followed bearing a loaded tray. "I was trying to persuade Nick to spend the night here, but he tells me he's already made arrangements to sleep aboard the mail boat."

"Captain Fergus wants to leave early in the morning and it seemed easiest that way. He has to deliver some loggers in time for their shift and he'll detour by Wickitak en route."

"Well, next time don't make any arrangements like that," Lennie admonished him. "I haven't even had a chance to ask you how your trip was."

"Very nice." Nick was passing generous pieces of pecan pie and distributing cups and saucers. "I'm glad you remembered the whipped cream, Lennie."

"You don't need whipped cream with pecan pie," Sue said. "It's loaded with calories already."

"*You* may not need it," he pointed out politely, "but I certainly do." He picked up his fork. "And if you're going to talk any more about calories, I'll call a cab to take you back to the hotel right now."

"I apologize." Sue smiled across at Lennie. "This looks so good, I'll be racing him to the kitchen for a second piece."

"Then you'd better start eating." Lennie sipped at her coffee. "Nick tells me that you're Tim Strathern's niece. I've known your uncle for years. It seems strange we haven't met before."

"I don't get up this way too often. When I do, I usually stick pretty close to the lodge. Things were getting a little hectic there, so I treated myself to a weekend in town."

Nick choked slightly on being called "a hectic thing" but turned a bland eye toward her. He explained for Lennie's benefit. "Sue has three end-of-the-season guests."

"That's why I was so grateful when Nick came to work," Sue explained.

Lennie's eyebrows shot up as she looked at Nick. "You're working at Wickitak? I thought you were just taking a rest. So did Florence."

He looked blank. "Who's Florence?"

"Florence Davis, of course," Lennie said impatiently. "I met her downtown today. She was telling me all about their stay at the lodge."

"How the devil do you know her?"

"Good heavens, man, she was one of the most important women up in this part of the country until she went south to live about ten years ago."

"Important? In what way?"

Lennie waved her fork in a graphic gesture. "Well—money, I suppose. Actually she came up here as a schoolteacher, but she soon went on to more lucrative things. First off, she married a miner named McCauley who had the good sense to die a few years later. Florence took his grubstake and started investing in real estate here. That was when she really hit the jackpot." She turned to Sue and explained. "You see, when Alaska became a state in 1959, more than 99 percent of the land 'belonged' to the federal government. That meant a person could always turn a tidy profit on the privately owned pieces. Florence wasn't too persnickety in how she achieved results. A lot of folks claimed that she just waited until they got in a jam financially before she stepped in and bailed them out—at a nice profit, of course."

"It's funny I never heard of her," Nick muttered.

"It's not funny at all. For one thing, she did

most of her dealing under her husband's name. She just took her maiden name back a few years ago." Lennie fixed him with an admonishing eye. "When you've visited me lately, you had other things on your mind." She let the pause lengthen. "Now that you've got a new job, I'm surprised you have time for your old friends at all."

His look was sardonic. "If you didn't make such good pie, I would have crossed you off my visiting list years ago. Go on—about Florence."

"There's not much more to tell. After a while, her reputation got a little too tarnished for most folks and she took off for a state with more sunshine. At least, that's what I heard." She pursed her lips thoughtfully. "I wouldn't be surprised if she'd kept her hand in with developments up here. Ever since there's been all that publicity over the big money changing hands on those Prudhoe Bay oil leases, Alaska has attracted lots of folks."

She moved over to pick up the poker and push back a log in the fireplace. "I'll tell you this much, Nick . . . if you have any money dealings with Florence, hang onto your wallet. On any other subject, she's as pleasant a woman as you could hope to meet."

"She's certainly been quiet about having lived here before," Sue said, frowning. "From the way she acted, I would have sworn she was a brand-new tourist."

"I wonder what she's up to?" Lennie's tone was pensive. "Florence was never one to do silly things. Always pretty levelheaded and direct."

"That's more than I can say for her neurotic nephew," Sue told her. "He's a walking medical case history; he possesses every symptom in the books."

"And Sue's heard them all." Nick was pursuing the last crumb of piecrust on his plate. "At least Monica's perfectly healthy."

"Very healthy," Sue said sarcastically. "If you mean she has all her red corpuscles. I'm not so sure about the balance of her libido."

He just grinned.

"Who's Monica?" Lennie asked.

"The gorgeous brunette secretary that Florence's nephew has in tow," Sue informed her. "Every man reacts to her like a Roman candle."

"What about women?"

"The path behind her is strewn with their fallen bodies."

"You'll notice I'm not saying a word," Nick said virtuously.

"You always were too darned closemouthed, Nicholas," Lennie complained, taking another sip of coffee. "It's a good thing you have some friends around to do your bragging. Florence was real interested when I told her all about you."

"Hell!" Nick put his plate back on the tray

with more force than necessary. "I'll bet she was."

Sue's eyes widened. "What's all this? You'll have to clue me in."

"I'm sorry, Nick," Lennie said in a worried tone. "Have I done something wrong?"

He raked impatient fingers through his hair. "Of course not. This news about Florence caught me off-balance, but I'm sorry I exploded. It's too late for her to cause any trouble now." His attention gravitated to Sue's quiet form. "I'd rather not explain right this minute—I'll tell you all about it in a day or so. Both of you," he amended.

"All right. We'll talk about it then." Lennie leaned forward to refill his coffee cup. "It's time we changed the subject anyway. What a pity you won't be here in the morning to see our new chapel out at Auke Bay."

"Finally got it finished, did you?"

She nodded. "Now I'm involved in arranging flowers for the altar instead of worrying about the building fund." She turned to Sue. "Perhaps you'd like to go out for the early service."

"I would if I can get back in time for a fairly early takeoff."

"You fly with Cal Martin, don't you?"

"Yes . . . do you know him?"

The other's eyes twinkled. "Everybody knows Cal; he's a popular young man."

"And a nice one," Sue defended staunchly. "My uncle thinks the world of him."

"So do I," Lennie said. "He's my godson and I feel a special responsibility for him. I just hope that he'll settle down with a nice girl one of these days." She tilted her head and peered over at Sue like an inquisitive bird. "Maybe you're the one he needs."

"Stop probing, Lennie," Nick growled.

"Why? Don't you know that poking my nose in other people's affairs is the most fun I get out of life these days?"

"Affair is the wrong word, Mrs. Brock," Sue said lightly. "With Cal, call it propinquity. At the moment, he's intrigued with Monica."

"Pshaw! She doesn't sound like the lasting type. Now you—you're different." She nodded briskly as if that put an end to the matter.

"Don't let her stampede you," Nick advised Sue. "I should have warned you that under that angelic exterior there's the drive of a longshoreman."

"And occasionally the vocabulary of one," Lennie admitted.

"I'm not stampeded," Sue said, smiling at the older woman. "Anyone who can bake a pecan pie like this can be as eccentric as she likes."

"Good girl. I'll pick you up at your hotel in plenty of time for the nine o'clock service tomorrow morning if that's all right."

"That will be fine, thank you."

The rest of the evening progressed along more orthodox conversational lines. Lennie delighted Sue by opening her glass-fronted cabinets filled with Indian and Eskimo treasures and telling some of the stories concerning them. It wasn't until she reached the final piece, a beautifully carved ivory chin drill, that the older woman noted Nick's preoccupation.

"Goodness, Nick—you haven't said a word for an hour. I didn't mean to bore you with the same old stories," she said apologetically.

"You couldn't bore me if you tried, Lennie," he told her definitely. "Chalk my bad manners up to a lack of sleep."

Sue's eyebrows climbed slightly. So Nick was finding sleep difficult too. She sneaked a fleeting glance and then sighed softly. From the impassive expression on his face, she decided he wasn't going to furnish any reasons for his insomnia either. Obviously the man was directly descended from the sphinx!

The sphinx chose that moment to say, "I'm afraid we'd better be going...."

Sue looked at her watch. "Heavens yes—otherwise I'll never make early church. I didn't realize it was so late."

Lennie closed the glass-fronted cabinet and put an arm around Sue's waist. "Both of you must come back soon and we'll have a proper dinner. I'll call you at the hotel tomorrow morning, Sue, when I'm ready to leave the house. We can have a fine gossip about Nick when he isn't around."

"I can only hope," he told them severely, "that there's a confession during the service."

"There always is," Lennie said in a serene voice.

The cab ride back down the hill was brief and accomplished with a climactic squeal of brakes when the driver pulled up in front of Sue's hotel.

"My god, that guy must have trained on the Hollywood freeway," Nick muttered as the man bounded around the car to open the door for them.

"Or the Grand Prix de Monaco," she agreed shakily, climbing out. "He's wasting his talents here." She pushed her hair back from her face. "At least we made it."

"Ummm." He took her hand briefly as she paused on the sidewalk. "Thanks for the evening. . . . I'll see you back at the lodge tomorrow."

She took a deep breath and tried to cover her disappointment at his abrupt leave-taking. "Of course, Nick. Thanks for wining and dining me. And I enjoyed meeting Lennie."

There was a long look and a muscle pulsed in his jaw before he said softly, "Good night, my dear. Don't forget to come home."

By the time those quiet words penetrated her consciousness, he had stepped back into the cab and the driver had taken off.

Chapter Seven

The memory of those soft-spoken words buoyed Sue's mood through the rest of the night and the next morning in the beautifully situated chapel by the lake at Auke Bay. With its wall of glass behind the altar, the well-known log church personified the close existence with nature shared by all Alaskans. The towering hills and the quiet waters of the lake were a living testimony to the grandeur in their outer lives, the simple worship service a reflection of their inner ones.

Even meeting the "terrible trio" for the trip back to the lodge couldn't dull Sue's enchantment with the day. Her mind was on Nick, first and foremost, and every minute that passed brought her closer to him.

Cal observed her preoccupation and diagnosed it with masculine perception. He didn't say anything until after they had set down by the boathouse and watched Florence, Monica, and Leo start up the path.

"I'll carry your bag up for you," he said.

"Thanks, but it isn't necessary. I imagine Nick will be down to do it." Her tone was absentminded but there was nothing distracted about her glance up the path. Obviously she was looking for the tall figure of a temporary caretaker.

"What gives with him anyhow?" Cal's dislike was evident.

"What on earth do you mean?"

"Don't play the innocent with me—he isn't the caretaker type." He stuck his hands in his pockets belligerently. "I heard you were out with him last night."

"It's hardly a secret. I ran into him in the museum yesterday afternoon."

"That's what I mean—since when do general handymen hang around in those places?"

She kneaded the shoulder strap of her bag between her thumb and forefinger aimlessly. "Now you're being absurd. You can't tell a man's interests these days by the kind of job he chooses. Maybe Nick's different in his choice of hobbies."

"At least you think so," he said hotly. "You should have told me the other night before I made a fool of myself."

"You didn't make a fool of yourself. . . ."

"The hell I didn't!" He reached up and started vigorously rearranging the freight stowed behind the seats of the plane. "Evidently I'm not the only one." The words were muttered but distinct.

"I don't like your cryptic remarks." Sue's patience with him in this mood was about exhausted. "If you have something to say—say it."

He stepped back, looking ill at ease as he rubbed off some grime on his shirt. "Look, Sue ... I don't want to fight with you. Are you sure I can't interest you in that proposition I made at the hotel? We get along just fine most of the time."

"Getting along just fine isn't enough," she assured him with her new-found knowledge.

"If I didn't care about you, it wouldn't matter if this guy Dunbar was hanging around. Don't you see—I don't want you to get hurt!"

She pushed back a strand of hair with a distrait hand. "I wish to heaven you'd stop slinging innuendoes or casting aspersions or whatever it is you're doing. Just how is having Nick on the premises going to hurt me?"

"I don't trust him. I don't think you should trust him." He put up his hand to forestall an interruption. "Before you get all het up, ask him why he's hanging around Wickitak?"

"He works here ... remember? I suppose he needed a job for the moment, so he answered my ad."

He shook his head pityingly. "That's what I mean ... you're being led up the garden path, Sue. You've got so many stars in your eyes that you can't see the truth." He reached out for her hand. "Listen, and listen carefully. I had coffee yesterday afternoon with the gal who works in the Juneau newspaper office. She wanted to know how you were managing up here. I couldn't see why she was so interested until she told me that they didn't have a single answer to that ad you put in the paper." He watched the anger fade from her features and a bleak look replace it. "They would have known about Dunbar. The applicants were only given a box number at the paper to write to and you didn't mention the name of the lodge." Her continued silence made him uneasy. "Look—" he blurted out, "just ask the guy how he heard about Wickitak, will you? It wouldn't be the first time a gal like you was courted for her tangible assets. Your uncle's pretty well-heeled."

"Thanks, Cal," she said quietly, pulling her hand away. "I'll remember what you've said."

"Oh God! . . . I didn't mean to hurt you. I'm sorry, Sue." He pulled her roughly against him and pressed his cheek to hers.

"Don't," she whispered when she could. She patted his shirt front unsteadily. "I'd better get out of here before I make a fool of myself for sure." She tipped her head back to kiss him lightly. "Goodbye, Cal . . . I'll be in touch."

He watched her start up the path and then noticed, up at the sharp bend of the trail above the boathouse, the onlooker to their farewell. He stared defiantly back at him for a long moment before turning his back as he climbed into the cockpit of the Cessna and slammed the door. "Get your answers ready, Dunbar," he muttered forcefully, reaching over to switch on, "you're going to need them."

Exactly the same thought was running through Sue's mind as she plunged up the path, her eyes still filled with tears after Cal's recital of home truths. There was a temptation to get out of sight and sort her thoughts before encountering anyone. Her blissful mood had been rudely shattered by the disclosure and she felt as much on the defensive as a wounded animal. And also as ready to strike out at anyone who got in her way.

It was especially unfortunate that it had to be Nick and that she had to literally careen into him because she wasn't looking where she was going. The impact sent her reeling and only his quick grasp at her arm maintained her balance.

"What's the matter?" His voice was as brusque as Cal's had been. "Was that sentimental farewell too much for you? Lennie was right—Cal Martin evidently has a way with him."

"He isn't the only one, is he?" Her pride flared up instantly at his sarcasm. She shook off his hand as if she couldn't bear his slightest touch. "At least Cal doesn't pretend to be anything he isn't. Why did you tell me that you'd seen that ad for a caretaker?"

His eyebrows jerked up at her temper. "I didn't. The assumption was all yours."

"That's one way of evading the issue. If I hadn't been such a fool, I would have realized before this. There were enough slip-ups. You mentioned a map showing the rear entrance to the gold shaft and there isn't one, is there?" She glanced up at him for confirmation. "You knew all about Uncle Tim being at the Maputo Game Reserve in Mozambique. That bothered me at the time. It was as if you had inside information on everything." She pulled down her voice level with an effort. "Why did you come to Wickitak in the first place?"

"I wanted to keep an eye on the property ... and you," he said evenly.

"You've one hell of a nerve...."

"Maybe. You wanted the truth ... now you have it. Take it from there."

Her eyes narrowed at his insouciance. "What's this about property? Lennie was talking about Florence and property last night."

"That's right." His jaw tightened at her suspicious look. "There's no point in beating around the bush. We both want the same piece. I plan to get it. Florence can make other plans."

"Who does it belong to now?"

"Your uncle. Until eight o'clock tomorrow morning."

Her mouth dropped open. "And you have

the ... unmitigated gall ... to stand there and admit you've been hanging around here ... accepting a salary check ... while you're calmly planning to filch Uncle Tim's property!"

"If you'll pipe down for a minute I can explain...."

"Don't bother." Her tone indicated that even being in the same state with him was bad enough. "Collect your things and get out of here today. I'll pay for the charter gladly."

"Stop being a damn fool and listen ... even Monica knows when to stop acting like a nincompoop! I don't have time to explain everything now ... you'll have to take it on trust."

She broke in explosively, "You must be out of your mind."

"I'm right up to the wire on time," he said, ignoring her outburst completely. "And today's the only day I have left to check that land. I'm depending on you to keep Florence and Leo down here out of harm's way." He smacked a violent fist into his palm. "Damn! If they've changed those blazes or moved any stakes, they could have undone a month's work."

"I don't know what you're talking about...."

"And I've told you that doesn't matter ... now. You can have the whole explanation later—wrapped up in blue ribbons if you want it. Just believe me when I tell you that this is the way your uncle wants it."

Sue's eyes widened at his final words. "Let's

suppose for a minute that I believe your story," she said slowly. "How am I supposed to keep them occupied?"

"Damned if I know. Sidetrack Leo with a discussion of his symptoms if you have to."

"That's not going to excite Monica for long, or Florence either," she informed him absently. Her main train of thought was wondering what had happened to the polite, slow-moving man who had brushed off irritations as she would brush off a fly. Hearing his cold, implacable voice now, she realized that his detached manner had been strictly top layer; underneath he was as impenetrable and rugged as polished steel.

"I'm leaving right now," he continued. "It's a long hike, but I'll be back before dark with any luck. There wouldn't be any problem if the jeep were operating. As it is, I'll cut across the glacier to save time."

"Glissading across that ice can be tricky," she pointed out. "I hope you know what you're doing."

His smile was bleak. "If I don't, then it will be your turn to come and rescue me."

"I'm serious. Even experienced mountaineers come to grief on those pressure ridges."

"Don't worry, I'll watch my step. Besides, it's just a short trek across the ice. If I'm not back by dark, send Rock out with a keg of brandy around his neck."

"I could always send Monica instead."

"Another time, thanks. Monica's ideas on rescue work wouldn't coincide with mine."

"Then Marie and I will have to hogtie her for the rest of the day."

"You won't have Marie to help. . . ."

"Oh?"

"She took off with Fergus on the mail boat. He brought her a message from the hospital . . . some kind of trouble with Joe."

"I don't understand. He was doing just fine when I called the hospital yesterday."

His forehead furrowed with a sudden, savage scowl. "What the devil is going on, do you suppose? I'm not sure it's a good idea to leave you here alone with them."

"There isn't any choice. I'd look all kinds of a fool calling Cal back strictly on intuition." She gave him a puzzled look. "How are you going to get down to Juneau tomorrow morning? Cal didn't say anything about making a trip to pick you up."

There was a surge of red under the skin on his cheekbones. "I made arrangements with one of his competitors. From the look he gave me a few minutes ago, it's just as well I did. I have a feeling that otherwise I'd have been invited to jump without a parachute right over the main channel."

She nodded. "He thinks you're up to no darned good."

"And you? What do you *really* think?" For the first time his voice softened.

There was no evading that piercing glance. She stared back at him, her eyes full of undeclared love.

"What difference does it make?" She tried to laugh. "Besides, when it comes to choosing between you and Leo . . ."

She broke off in midsentence as he groaned and yanked her against him hard . . . then firm lips were parting hers. There was determination and desperation in that kiss—as well as a great deal more.

Surprise made her rigid for an instant until the warm burgeoning of desire caused her to melt against him, her arms stealing up to circle his neck.

It was some time before he pushed her reluctantly away.

"I've been wanting to do that," he said unevenly, "ever since that morning when I first saw you on the path with the sun shining down on you. It's been hell keeping away."

"You certainly didn't give that impression." Her erratic breathing matched his. She risked a shy glance upward. "When I had that nightmare, you couldn't have been more casual . . . or disinterested. Telling me to forget everything that happened . . ." she traced a wavering line down his cheek with a slender finger . . . "when I wanted to cry on your shoulder."

He captured the finger and held it tight. "I knew very well what you wanted. It seemed a hell of a lot better if I didn't clue you in on *my* feelings just then. Don't forget . . . we were alone in the lodge and you'd had a devil of a day. Any man who'd take advantage of a woman under those circumstances would be a four-star heel." He smiled whimsically down on her. "Retreat seemed the order of the day—and night. Being stiff-necked and pompous was the best way of getting out of that bedroom without completely giving myself away."

"I didn't know. . . ."

His hands moved up to her shoulders and shook them gently. "If you hadn't acted like a cretin, you could have figured it out. Cal Martin did. Incidentally, no more romantic farewells with your favorite pilot or I'll dump *him* into midchannel without a parachute."

She said softly, "You didn't seem like the jealous type."

He gave her a rueful glance before flicking the end of her nose with his finger. "I wasn't . . . until I saw you. There's a first time for everything." His hands dropped purposefully. "Damn—if I don't get going, I won't make it back before dark."

"Nick—please be careful." She caught at the sleeve of his jacket. "The animals are coming down lower for food at this season. There's been so much rain this summer that the berries they feed on haven't ripened properly. I heard bears were foraging on the porch of a house in Juneau last night."

"They won't bother me," he assured her.

"But what about food for you? You should take some provisions."

"I have a couple of candy bars in my pocket—they'll tide me over until I get back. I don't want to stop and pack a lunch in the kitchen now; it's better to be on the way before Florence and Leo know I've gone." He pulled her close against him for a moment while he rested his cheek against her soft hair. "Sue dear—take care," his voice was deep. "I'll be thinking about you." Then he turned her around smartly so that she was facing up the path. "Now—march!"

She nodded silently. Her hand reached back to grasp his for a fleeting instant before she pulled it away and hurried up the path out of sight.

As she went along, her heart pounded harder than the simple climb warranted. Her head was giddy, her vision blurred, and her breathing came in uneven jerks. There was also a decided urge to skip to the top of the hill and sing out with happiness. She smiled tremulously as she acknowledged she was well and truly smitten—fathoms deep in love.

Her smile widened. At least it wasn't a hopeless case as she had feared. Nick had clearly indicated that he felt the same way. True, he hadn't said anything definite—her heart gave a double thump at that—but things looked promising for the future. She remembered the passion in his kiss—as her heartbeat went up alarmingly again—and decided that promising was definitely the wrong word. Heavenly was far better. Far, far better.

Rock exploded off the porch of the lodge when he saw her coming and catapulted onto her, vibrating with glee. The rubber mallet he was carrying was dropped casually into a shrub as he found it necessary to express his complete happiness with sharp whines and a staccato series of barks.

"Stop it, silly," she commanded ineffectually, "or I'll need a towel to dry off." She sat down on the steps and hugged his shaggy head. "I brought you a present if you'll let me get it out of my purse."

The sound of paper rustling in the depths of her bag inspired the long Airedale nose to poke down and help.

"Hey... just a minute," she reproved. "Don't eat it... yet."

With his enthusiastic help, the paper bag was soon in shreds in her lap and Rock was throwing the rubber bone under the shrubbery and retrieving it with full-throated barks of glee.

"I wondered what all the commotion was about." Monica stood at the top of the porch steps with the front door open behind her. She pulled a package of cigarettes out of her skirt pocket and selected one carefully. "We'd like our bags or is self-service the rule of the day around here?"

"Of course not."

"I didn't think it was." The secretary gave Sue a sardonic look. "Not at your uncle's prices. Even if he gave away trading stamps, the tariff for this place makes Palm Springs a positive bargain."

Sue's first impulse was to suggest taking the first plane south, but she dutifully swallowed the words and instead said meekly, "I'm sorry you've been inconvenienced—I'm afraid you're not seeing the lodge at its best."

"I don't know about that," the other told her coolly. "There are certain side benefits to the place. You've managed to surround yourself with two of them."

Sue snapped the clasp on her purse with great care. "I'm not sure I follow you. . . ."

"Then you're dimmer than I thought." Monica's light tone made it hard to take offense. "I mean your pilot friend and Nick, of course. It doesn't look as if you're struggling very hard to keep either one of them."

Since Sue's heart was still thumping in double time as a result of Nick's final embrace, she was tempted to break out laughing at Monica's words. Her lips did quirk in amusement but she only said mildly, "I thought the man was the one who did the struggling."

The other narrowed her eyes thoughtfully. "Either you're incredibly naive or smarter than I'm giving you credit for."

Sue reached over to retrieve Rock's bone from the middle of a bushy shrub. "Better make it incredibly naive," she told Monica. "I didn't even know we were having a competition."

"If you'll cast your mind back to the hotel, you'll remember that you weren't outstandingly successful on one occasion."

"Golly," Sue said in assumed regret, "and I thought Leo and I had gotten along so well that night." Her gaze didn't flicker at Monica's snort of disgust. "Don't worry about your bags, though. I'll have them brought up right away."

"I suppose Nick can do it," the other said offhandedly. Then, more sharply, "He is around, isn't he?"

"Of course." She watched Monica stride back into the lodge and added sweetly, "Around a half-mile away if he's on schedule."

Watching Rock romp with his new toy gave her an excuse for standing there in a state of indecision. If she brought up the luggage in three separate trips and left it by the back door, Nick's departure would be covered for another hour or so. By the time lunch was prepared, his absence wouldn't matter. Even if Leo were to follow then, he wouldn't be able to make any difference in Nick's reconnaissance—the distance involved was too great.

Thoughtfully she whistled for Rock and waited for him to bound up beside her before going around to the back of the lodge. As she passed Florence's half-carved totem on the porch, she grinned. No wonder the woman had encountered so much trouble playing the heavy hobbyist. If real estate was her line, she should have settled for rock collecting and skipped some of the pitfalls. The grin faded as she remembered Lennie's stories of how the other had amassed her fortune. Probably everything about Alaska was as familiar to her as a crosstown bus was to Sue. How she must have laughed at their attempts to explain Alaskan Indian history.

Sue's footsteps slowed as her thoughts deepened. A woman who went to that much trouble to be on the scene wasn't going to give up easily. She administered a sharp mental shake to her feeling of sudden depression and walked purposefully on. Nick was depending on her, after all, and it was no time to go into a blue funk.

It wasn't until she had made a third trip back

up the hill and dropped the last two bags by the kitchen door that she noticed the difference; chips were still scattered on the porch and the chunky base was still in its place—only Florence's totem had been taken away. She stood quietly for a moment, trying to think what that removal could mean. Unless she was to find the totem stacked in the lodge's log rack, Florence evidently planned to take it with her. Following that reasoning, it would mean the three of them were planning to leave considerably sooner than they had proclaimed.

She bit down hard on her lower lip to still its trembling. Nick had mentioned eight o'clock tomorrow morning as his deadline. From the look of things, Florence wasn't interested in overland pursuit, so she must have another plan in mind.

It was lunchtime before the first possible tip-off came. They had all gathered in seeming harmony over the buffet of cold meats and salads that Marie had left. When Florence asked if Nick were going to join them, Sue's reply that "he was trying to clear a trail and probably wouldn't be back until late afternoon" didn't cause a ripple.

Florence picked up a plate and weighed the merits of baked ham against pastrami. "Well then, there's no point in waiting for him, is there? We were hoping to go out for some fishing this afternoon, but I think Leo and

Monica can handle the boat all right." She frowned as she glanced across at Sue. "Unless you'd like to come along. Probably you'd feel easier about things then."

Sue thought fast. Evidently they had decided that she was safer under their eyes than waiting at the lodge for Nick. "Whichever you prefer," she told Florence finally. "If you want the cruiser, I'd better go down and get it ready. Uncle Tim doesn't let it go out unless both fuel tanks are full. We won't need the reserve but he feels it's safer."

"I could do that," Leo said halfheartedly, obviously torn between gallantry and the potato salad. "You must be hungry."

She shook her head. "I had a sandwich in the kitchen when I was transferring the contents of the refrigerator. It won't take me long to check the cruiser and then we'll be ready to go right after you've finished lunch."

"How thoughtful of you, dear." Florence shook out her napkin and surveyed her heaped plate. "There's something about this northern air that ruins any thoughts I had about dieting. You run along then. We'll save some coffee for you."

Sue glanced at her watch as she went out the back door and kept a sedate pace on the path until she was out of sight of the lodge. Then she broke into a trot, which delighted Rock who was keeping her company. He barked sharply and nearly caused her to fall flat as he dashed in front of her. "Quiet, boy," she told him. "You can make yourself useful by going on guard duty when we get down to the boathouse. This is one time when I don't want to be interrupted."

Fortunately, refueling the cruiser went off smoothly and it was barely a half hour later that she was rejoining the trio in the spacious lounge, where they were sitting over coffee.

"Everything's ready," she told them blithely. "I can't promise to find all the good fishing spots, but we should hit a few."

"Good!" Florence was cheerful. "Sit down and have some coffee. I like some insulation before I get chilled out on the water. Leo ..." she raised her voice and he looked across from his perch on a bar stool beside Monica, "bring Sue some coffee."

"Sure, Flo." He shuffled over to the coffee urn at the end of the bar and took a mug from the stack alongside. He filled it plus a serving pitcher and arranged them both on a tray. That was hoisted carefully in front of him and brought across to where they were sitting on the wide divan. "I wasn't sure what you liked in yours, but there's cream and sugar," he told Sue.

"Thanks—I'll help myself." She sugared her coffee and then used a generous amount of cream. "My uncle has a fit when he sees me do that," she confessed. "He says the only way to drink coffee is black and strong."

"I suppose most men feel that way." Florence refilled her mug from the server while her nephew moved back to the bar. Apparently Leo's gallantry appeared only at specific requests.

Sue noticed the older woman craning her head to decipher a motto embroidered on the tray cloth. "You can never be too rich or too thin," she translated for her. "Marie loves to embroider and the linen closet is full of towels saying things like 'The hurrier I go, the behinder I get' or 'Yard by yard, life is hard.' I think the prize of her collection is a hand towel which warns you that 'Of all sad deaths, the very worst is that which comes from burning thirst.'"

Monica had turned to stare. "Charming ... but hardly appropriate for the weather in this part of the country. How about 'Rain ... rain, go away. ...'"

Sue smiled. "I'll suggest it to Marie."

"Your uncle should have a motto carved on the edge of that magnificent mantel," Florence said, indicating the fireplace in front of them.

"I'll tell him when he gets back." Sue took another swallow of coffee. "What do you suggest? Something like Kipling's 'This is the law of the jungle'? No—that's more for Africa, isn't it?" She turned to Florence. "What would you put there?"

The other looked at her enigmatically. "There's one saying that I've lived by all my life . . . 'Necessity has no law.' Rabelais said it."

"I don't think Uncle Tim would approve of that," Sue said definitely.

"I'm sure he wouldn't—but then he didn't approve of me years ago." Florence was complacent. "He turned me down flat when I made an offer for this lodge after my husband died. He also made a few scathing remarks about women not being fitted to handle an operation of this kind. That's where he was wrong, though—I could handle anything I decided to set my mind to." She cradled her coffee mug in square, capable hands. "I went on to prove him wrong; I made twice as much money in real estate as Tim ever thought of making. Later on, he saw fit to tell me he didn't approve of some of my dealings. That's why I knew he wouldn't agree to any arrangement of mine on that land of his that both Nick and I want."

Sue blinked owlishly. Florence was taking the gloves off with a vengeance and she felt barely able to take it in. Perhaps another swallow of hot coffee would help wake her up.

Florence smoothed a wrinkle in her skirt and went on complacently. "When I heard Nick's company had sent him out to Mozambique to talk to Tim after their survey, I decided that I'd better get closer to the scene of action."

"I didn't know that he had actually seen my uncle...."

"Oh yes. That's when he pursuaded Tim not to take up his option." Her lips thinned reprovingly. "I'd like to know how he pursuaded Tim to do that."

Sue noted that both Leo and Monica had dropped all pretense of conversation and were listening to Florence.

"Of course, since his company has the government contracts, he might have pulled in a patriotic angle." The older woman's face flushed as she showed the first vestige of emotion. "Tim's a fool! He could have made a fortune on that land if he'd gone in with me."

"I don't understand at all." Sue waggled her head groggily. "What's this about Nick's company? I thought he was between jobs." She heard Leo snort in the background. "I did," she insisted staunchily. "He didn't say anything when he applied for a job here."

"Well, you certainly have one of the highest-salaried caretakers in this part of the world," Florence said wryly. "I doubt if he'll ever have to wonder where his next meal is coming from. He's a cadastral engineer among other things, quite a talented person."

"What's a cad . . . cadastra . . . ?" Sue gave up and tried to focus on the figure beside her. As it blurred, she reached up to cool her hot cheeks with the backs of her hands. What in the world had happened to her?

"A cadastral engineer is one who determines the extent and value of land." She could hear Florence going on like a schoolteacher again. "And Nick is very good at his job. He made a mistake though, in counting out any opposition. If I can register my claim for that piece of land tomorrow morning before he does, then Nick's employers will have to deal with me."

"And Aunt Florence can be damned expensive," Leo put in.

Florence waved him to silence. "That's enough, Leo. This isn't the time for patting ourselves on the back. I want Sue to listen carefully while she can still understand. When Nick gets back this afternoon, he'll find that it will be impossible for him to get to Juneau tomorrow morning."

"But there's a pilot coming," Sue protested with an effort.

"He'll be a couple of hours late," Monica said smugly and then broke off as Florence shot her a quelling look.

"Just take my word for it," the older woman said briskly, turning back to Sue. "I expect to pay for any damage we incur. I'll leave my lawyer's address and you can forward the bills. Naturally, if you try to file any sort of criminal action, I'll deny the whole thing. The cruiser will be left at the transient dock in the boat harbor north of Juneau. I think that covers everything."

Sue's head felt too heavy to support any longer. She struggled to remain sitting upright. "Wha ... what ... have ... you ... done ... to ... me?" The words came out laboriously and so low that the others had to strain to hear them.

"Nothing that won't wear off in a few hours." Florence was completely dispassionate. "We talked it over and decided that it would be more convenient to leave you here than to confine you on the boat. I detest having to use force—a little nap is far more civilized. Leo merely laced your coffee with two of his sleeping pills ... he thought that should do it. I do hope his dosage is right."

Florence's sudden frown was the last thing Sue saw before her eyelids came down like a heavy black cloud. The last words she breathed were, "Oh God—so do I!"

Chapter Eight

It was dampness that brought about Sue's return to consciousness hours later. Dripping, soggy, sloshing dampness.

There had been a slight urge to lift her heavy eyelids before, but the lethargy that lined her bones prevented it. She might have slept on indefinitely if something moist, chilly, and impatient hadn't been jamming into her cheek and forehead. The last time the damp prodding was accompanied by a whine that acted like a cold shower on her memory.

"Rock!"

Her eyelids flew open and she struggled up from the davenport, where she had collapsed face down. The big Airedale whined again and put his front paws up on the cushion beside her, his whole body vibrating from his wagging tail.

"Oh lord—I feel awful!" She leaned her forehead against his massive shoulder until the room stopped revolving around her. Then she pulled away as her memory came flooding back. Her distracted glance shot around the spacious lounge. The room was deserted; only the scattered coffee mugs revealed that there had been other occupants.

She pushed Rock down on the floor and tried to focus on her watch. Finally she had to struggle to her feet and move nearer the window before she could see the time. Five-thirty! She'd been asleep for hours—no wonder Rock had been trying to make her stir.

Her head throbbed with the grandfather of all headaches and she leaned against the long window to cool her forehead. Thanks to Leo's miserable pills, her mental processes were still functioning at half-speed.

She widened her eyes with an effort and stared out into the gathering dusk. Nick should be back by this time. He'd had plenty of time to make the round trip unless he'd run into some trouble. She felt the impact of that thought sink in. There could be plenty of trouble on that trail. Even with slowed reasoning powers, she knew that.

If he didn't get back by dark—and her mind strove to remain logical and not panic—he'd be in for a cold, uncomfortable night. If he had hit trouble crossing the glacier and was stranded on the ice. . . . At that point, her mind rebelled and a moan escaped her lips, causing Rock to abandon his search for crumbs and come over to stand beside her.

She pulled his ear absently. The only thing to do was consider all the possibilities for help.

Obviously, the cruiser would be gone; the jeep didn't work, the radio. . . .

But Florence wouldn't have left a functioning radio, she reasoned. Nevertheless, it wouldn't hurt to check.

She stumbled up the stairs and shoved open the door to Uncle Tim's study only to pull up short. Florence had certainly taken no chances. The pitiful state of the radio's remains made her seethe with anger. She saw a small white card in the middle of her uncle's desk blotter and leaned over to read the name and address of an upright firm of Juneau attorneys. So those were the men who would handle Florence's financial dealings.

"Damn . . . damn . . . damn!" she whispered and wandered over to the study window. Cal wouldn't be unduly worried when she didn't get in touch at their usual evening call time. He *would* be alarmed when he couldn't contact her in the morning, but by then it would be too late! Nick had said eight o'clock, and if he couldn't make the deadline—there was little doubt that Florence would.

She stopped in her bathroom just long enough to splash icy water on her face and run a comb through her hair before hurrying down the hallway to check the condition of the three-room suite. One look . . . and she could heave a sigh of relief. Evidently their deliberate destruction had been limited to the radio. Florence's room was almost pristine in is neatness and the only evidence of Leo's occupancy was an empty cough-drop box. Monica's sole bequest was a cosmetic trail of spilled loose powder on the dressing table.

The bed linen in all the rooms was immaculate; mute testimony to Marie's housekeeping activity before their return.

Sue leaned against the door and tried to pull her chaotic thoughts back into line. If Florence had decreed that vandalism was to be kept at a minimum, there might just be a chance that they had left the dinghy in workable condition. It wasn't possible to carry enough fuel to achieve any great distance but at least she could get into midchannel and hail a fishing boat. The thought of battling treacherous currents in the small boat made her mind panic again. It was time, she decided sternly, to get herself under control. And it was also time to get cracking!

She turned back into her bedroom to snatch a nylon parka from her closet before hurrying down the staircase and whistling for Rock to accompany her down the boathouse path. He came flying out of the kitchen with a green dog biscuit sticking jauntily from the corner of his mouth.

"This isn't a picnic, you crazy galoot," she admonished as he capered happily beside her. "You didn't have to bring a lunch along."

His acknowledgment was to toss the biscuit high and make a great production out of recovering it, tail wagging frantically all the while.

They slowed to a stop at the final bend of the path and Sue stared down on the apparently deserted boathouse. The door was standing ajar, the interior looming dark and forbidding.

"Come on, Rocko," she coaxed finally, wishing her head wouldn't continue to vibrate with every heartbeat. "Let's see what they've left us."

It took two more minutes and one step inside the building itself to realize that what Florence had left wasn't much. The berths where the cruiser and dinghy usually rested were mockingly empty. Evidently the trio had decided it was easier to tow the small boat and cut it adrift in the channel rather than risk damaging it. So scratch the use of one dinghy. The outboard was left hanging on its clamp. Probably they reasoned that one functioning outboard motor wasn't much use without a boat to go with it.

Sue wearily rubbed her throbbing head as she went back out into the dusk and leaned against the front of the building. There was no use evading the truth any longer. Not only had Nick's hopes been blasted for the land option, but he was now probably in actual trouble as well. The thought of his being in physical danger made her stomach muscles tighten and a nausea sweep over her.

How could she ever have doubted his attraction—even in the beginning? Now, when committed completely and powerless to help him, she became aware of the depth of that love.

Her unhappy gaze followed Rock, who was cavorting by the entrance to the carport. The sturdy Airedale was methodically flipping his dog biscuit into the air and then pouncing on it as it skittered along the ground.

"Look out," she warned him from force of habit, "or you'll lose it under the . . ." Her voice trailed off as she suddenly realized exactly what he would lose it under. "My lord," she breathed prayerfully, "the jeep!" In a second, she was tearing at that unwieldy tarp covering. "I'll bet they didn't even touch it," she was saying, "please . . . make it that they didn't touch it." Then the covering was bunched on the floor and she was stepping over it to stare at the dashboard. That wonderful, dirty, scratched, and well-worn dashboard with an untouched, functioning two-way radio mounted beneath it!

Pay dirt at last. Since the jeep wasn't movable, it obviously hadn't occurred to Florence to seek further. Sue shivered with sudden excitement; it almost hadn't occurred to her to seek further either. And what a blessing Leo hadn't bothered to look beyond the rear bumper the morning they walked to the mine.

She turned to the wall of the carport and pawed impatiently under a pile of waders for the flexible antenna which was always removed from the rear bumper mounting when the jeep was stored. Joe had methodically removed it as usual, Sue decided, so that it would clear the low, lean-to roof. An upright antenna would have been an automatic tip-off to the radio's existence.

The steel whip was being triumphantly hauled into the clear when she heard Rock's anguished whimper and noticed his frantic scratching in a nearby corner.

"I told you," she said accusingly as she dropped the antenna by the rear bumper of the jeep and stalked over to the unhappy dog. "Where did you throw your biscuit this time?" She knelt and watched him scrabble in a coil of nylon line which had evidently been knocked to the floor from the top of a narrow worktable.

"It would serve you right if I made you go without," she said severely. "Now—after I give it to you this time . . . take it outside . . . or eat it." She was coiling the line as she spoke. "There it is." She watched his eager wet nose nudge aside the last strand and pounce on the gummy green biscuit. "Remember what I said . . ." The words were strangled in her throat as she saw another find under the rope—a small piece of dirty brown plastic roughly shaped like the handle of a bathroom faucet.

She picked up the rotor from the distributor reverently, her fingers polishing the grimy surface while she swallowed mightily and tried to keep the tears under her eyelids from spilling down her cheeks. It was more than a miracle. It was as if the heavens had suddenly opened and dropped down a casual gift from the gods.

She clutched the piece of plastic even more tightly and moved over to the hood of the jeep. It took barely four minutes before the part was put in its proper place and the clamshell hood slammed back down. Scarcely daring to breathe, she got into the driver's seat and leaned forward to turn on the ignition switch. Her foot reached up for the starter pedal and the engine sputtered . . . caught . . . only to die immediately. She pressed down again and it roared into full-throated life.

This time the tears of joy did overflow as she backed the ancient vehicle out onto the track and carefully let the motor idle.

When it was running smoothly, she jumped out and whistled for Rock. "Come on, boy—quick! There's a lot to do and now every minute counts."

Despite her hurry, it was completely dark by the time she had loaded the back of the jeep to her satisfaction and driven out onto the mainland track.

The best possible chance to find Nick was by following it until it joined the trimline trail, which eventually disappeared into the side of the glacier. She recalled hearing her uncle tell how Alaskan trimline paths had gotten their names. Advancing glaciers had literally trimmed all vegetation from the land some two hundred years before, he had said. When the glaciers had finally retreated, the paths had become established among the fast-growing alder forests. Slow-melting blocks of ice became isolated during the recession and eventually melted to leave monumental depressions on the tracks which could be unnerving to an unwary driver.

She was thinking of those pitfalls as she drove carefully down the rutted track. When they combined with the potholes caused by surface water, all hope of speed was canceled. Not that there was much hope of speed in the old jeep anyhow, she acknowledged wryly, as they jounced along. Rock sat in the passenger seat beside her, his body still vibrating from the pleasure of being allowed to come. His solid bulk was reassuring when she remembered the rough trail she had to drive before reaching the glacier.

She smiled in satisfaction at the radio under the dashboard. The report to Cal had helped her morale immensely.

"Don't worry about Florence and her pals." His voice had come reassuringly from the speaker. "I'll alert the Coast Guard on the stolen cruiser."

"Tell them they probably won't get into Juneau tonight," she had said. "Actually I'll bet they don't want to appear until morning. There would be less chance of questions being asked if they turn up at the boat harbor at the last minute. After all, half of Juneau can identify that cruiser as Uncle Tim's property."

"Leave it to me," he promised. "I'll spread the word in case they do try to dock tonight. If they're anchored in a side channel somewhere, they may get a little cold—the temperature's nose-dived."

"I hope they freeze," she said forcefully. "When I think of how they calmly appropriated that boat and left me like Rip van Winkle on the couch . . ."

"Honey . . . I wish you'd stay that way. Wait until morning and I'll be up at the crack of dawn to help you look for Dunbar."

"I can't, Cal. You know the difference a few hours can make if he's been injured."

"Promise you won't do anything foolish like trying to search that ice until daylight."

She nodded, forgetting he couldn't see her. "I won't take any risks. There's a slim chance I can intercept him on the trail or in that old trapper's cabin by the side of the glacier. It wouldn't be the first time it's been used for emergencies."

"Okay. Drive carefully and check in with me after you've reached the cabin. Have you packed everything you need in the jeep?"

"Everything on the emergency list plus an eighty-pound Airedale."

"I wish it was a hundred-and-eighty-pound pilot."

"Stop it or you'll have me howling. I have to get going, Cal. I'll check with you in a couple of hours."

She came back to her immediate surroundings as Rock whined with excitement on the seat beside her. Abruptly, she yanked at the wheel to avoid hitting the fast-moving figure which flashed briefly in front of her headlights and then vanished. Her foot slammed the brake instinctively and then pulled up as the jeep fishtailed on the surface gravel and headed for the edge of the narrow road. There was a split second of panic before she regained control of the car and then she eased to a stop to regain control over her breathing as well. If she'd been six feet further along, there'd either be a Sitka deer in her lap by now or they'd both be lying side by side in the steep gully at the roadside. She shuddered and leaned over to rest her forehead on the clammy steering wheel. Rock whimpered and shifted to nuzzle her ear with his cold nose.

"Okay, my friend . . . we'll go . . . and thanks." She reached out a still-trembling hand to pat his head. "If we survive this, I don't plan to drive on anything smaller than an eight-lane freeway for the rest of my life. And then only in broad daylight." She watched him settle down again before she shifted into low and started up cautiously. "You're the watchdog," she reminded him firmly, "so for gosh sakes . . . watch!"

Her knuckles were white with strain by the time she turned onto the trimline trail. The broad river where Cal would put the Cessna down tomorrow morning was beyond sight down to the left. As it was partially fed by meltwater from deep within the glacier, its surface was often dotted by floating ice. Most of the bergs, though, would still be contained in the lake at the glacier face.

She drove steadily on, winding through the heavier Sitka spruce forest as the track circled away from the glacier for a half mile. It shouldn't be long now before reaching the cabin, she estimated.

Her spirits had sunk as the miles passed. Since Nick hadn't been on the main trail, her only hope was that he had sheltered in the hut.

Rock's warning whine was the first indication that they had reached their destination. Then the ruts of the road disappeared into bare terrain and she let the jeep slowly idle forward as she surveyed the dark cabin bathed in the glare of her headlights. Her teeth clamped down on her lower lip in sudden misery; she hadn't realized until then how she had been praying for lamplight through the hut's small window.

The jeep ground to a stop and she switched off the engine. Now there was only one remaining task—to tell Cal the bad news so that he could alert the rescue units.

Rock whined again and bounded to his feet on the seat.

"What is it, boy? What do you hear?" Suddenly uneasy, she strained to see around the side of the jeep and finally stared intently at the darkened shelter. This time, Rock's whine was relegated to the background as her headlight beam revealed the cabin door was ajar.

Her heartbeat bounded to double time . . . her mind rioted with possibilities. It wouldn't be the first time a wolf had found his way into a shelter or a curious bear—although the crack in the door looked pretty narrow for one of the latter. She hung onto Rock's collar to prevent any sudden departures on his part. The third possibility was Nick—and that meant no more sitting in the jeep and playing guessing games.

"Stay there, Rock!" she commanded and released his collar to press her thumb firmly on the horn button. The raucous sound vibrated through the night causing the Airedale to break into a volley of deep-throated barks.

In the middle of the commotion, Sue leaned out and pounded on the metal side of the jeep with the open palm of her other hand. Rock went into a new frenzy of barking and she grinned with satisfaction. That should be enough noise to send any animal scurrying!

But no gray shapes nor rotund ones appeared to slam that cabin door back in a frantic escape. She released the horn button and let silence descend. Rock was caught in the middle of a bark and turned to look sheepishly at her.

The interval lengthened—then she was rummaging at her side and pulling out a powerful battery lantern. There was only one sure way to find out what was in that cabin: go in and see for herself.

"Come on," she told the excited dog. "Heel!" She moved cautiously up to the building. Once at the door, she switched on the lantern and leaned over to push it further inward on creaking hinges.

Nothing happened.

She craned inside to flash the light on the dim interior. Its beam illuminated a crumpled heap on the floor on the first sweep and passed on. She yanked it back as she belatedly recognized it for what it was. Rock's rumbling growl changed into a sharp bark of excitement as he followed her sudden dash to the individual who was now struggling up on an elbow and blinking in the sudden light.

"Nick! Oh ... Nick!" She collapsed onto the dirty floor by his side, scarcely able to breathe in her searing relief. "I thought I'd lost you."

He shook his head. "I knew you'd get here ... sooner or later. But where in the devil have you been?" His voice sank to a mere thread and she had to bend down to hear the words. "You could always have sent Monica. ..."

Her lantern caught the weak grin on his weary face.

"Monica indeed!" Briefly, pithily, she told him exactly where he could go.

"I know ... I'll probably get there eventually." The grin had faded now and he caught at her hand. "Sue—for god's sake, darling, could we please stop off at Juneau tomorrow on the way."

With that request, he slid into unconsciousness at her feet.

Chapter Nine

Sue could only stare in horror at that limp, still form. Then she noticed the dark stain covering one shoulder of his quilted jacket and drew in her breath sharply as she leaned closer to examine it.

"Don't panic." Nick's eyelids had fluttered open again and he lay staring up at her. "I loused up my shoulder. It's nothing serious, but I couldn't get the damned thing to stop bleeding. Every time I move . . ." his voice broke off as he shifted position. "I could use some brandy if Rock brought any along."

"You lie still," she told him fiercely. "I have more than brandy in the back of the jeep and I'll have it unloaded in nothing flat." She watched him nod faintly and then close his eyes as if further conversation was beyond him just then.

"Rock . . . stay!" She left the lantern on the floor to provide illumination while she hurried out into the gleam of the headlights to start unloading. The radio contact with Cal would have to wait. First of all, she would bandage that shoulder of Nick's and make him more comfortable.

It took three trips before she had the gear unloaded and she was able to extinguish the headlights. She closed the cabin door firmly behind her and moved over by the fireplace to drop a bundle of kindling on the hearth.

"Maybe I can help. . . ." Nick was pushing up on an elbow again.

She rounded on him like a tigress. "Move another muscle and I'll have Rock stomp on you! You lie still, my friend." She turned back to the fireplace and wadded up an old newspaper from the pile next to a cache of firewood. "In a minute, we'll have some heat," she promised, arranging her cedar kindling carefully. "Joe tries to keep the cabin stocked with wood, but I thought it was safer to make sure. I'm such a horrible firemaker that I have to have all the conveniences—as you know." While she was chattering determinedly on, her hands were busy coaxing the small blaze to build until she could put on three good-sized logs. Then she sat back on her heels and surveyed the crackling fire with satisfaction. "There! That should warm things up."

"Good . . ." The words came out with an effort. "I was beginning to feel more like a slab of frozen fish each time I woke up."

"It's as well you managed to get off that glacier," she said solemnly, "or you'd be a slab of ice by now."

"Don't think that didn't occur to me."

She nodded, transferring the lantern to a rough table before checking the fuel level of a nearby kerosene lamp. "I'll light this later. Right now, I'd better find something comfortable for you to lie on."

"If you run across any innerspring mattresses, sling them over."

"Would you settle for the Alaskan equivalent?" She dragged over a rough frame which had been leaning against the wall. Leather thongs crisscrossed the top to make a rude, but serviceable camp bed. While he watched, she unrolled an air mattress and attached a foot pump to inflate it quickly.

"All the comforts of home," he observed through half-closed eyes.

"I learned about this on my first camping trip." She tested the buoyancy of the mattress before disconnecting the pump and then put her ear to the valve. "Good! Not a whisper." The mattress was arranged carefully over the thongs. She stood up straight and put her hands on her hips. "That should do for the moment." There was a sharp crack from the fire and a hot coal shot out onto the hearth. She moved over to kick it back in the flames with her boot before saying, "I have a sleeping bag over there to cover you later, but now I'd better take a look at that shoulder. I'll feel better when it's bandaged, and I think you will too." She knelt beside him. "Can you lever yourself up a few inches and slide on the cot? I'd rather you didn't try to stand up."

He managed a wry grin. "Coward!"

"You're darned right I am. Rock—stop being so curious!" She pushed the dog in the direction of the hearth. "Go over there and lie down." She turned to Nick again. "Once I get you up on it, I'll push it closer to the fire so you can get completely warm."

"Don't worry—I can manage."

He pushed up on his uninjured arm and then slid over to drape his upper torso on the bed. His face twisted in pain as he tried to lever himself onto it but by then Sue had caught hold of his boots and helped him manage the transfer. He lay still for a moment, his labored breathing sounding loud in the room.

Sue turned to rummage in the big first-aid box she had brought with her. "I have an ampul of ammonia here...."

"No, I'm all right now—thanks." The strained expression on his face smoothed away. "This is a terrific improvement over that floor."

"Nothing can beat the home comforts." She was assembling a thick compress and a roll of bandage. "If you hold still, I can unzip that jacket of yours and slip it off without too much trouble. You'll need it in the jeep tomorrow morning when we go down to meet Cal." Her hands were moving deftly as she spoke.

"So I did hear a car horn. I thought I'd wandered into one of your nightmares."

"Nope. Rock and I were trying to find out if any of our furry friends were in occupancy before we came calling. There!" She slid the jacket away triumphantly and reached for a pair of bandage scissors. "I hope you aren't too attached to this shirt because it will have to be cut away. Now—lie flat on your stomach. . . ." she paused and peered anxiously up at him. "Do you want a pillow?"

"Don't tell me you brought one?"

"Certainly. It only takes a minute to blow it up."

"Not now, thanks. I'm fine." He raised his eyebrows. "No caviar?"

"No caviar—but hot soup and vacuum jars of tea and coffee." She was cutting the flannel shirt carefully. "There's even a flask of brandy, which you cannot have until I get this bandaged." She intercepted an expressive glance. "I might need some cooperation, and brandy on an empty stomach. . . ." She shook her head. "I don't want you that relaxed ... thanks very much."

"You've got a point. Hey, I feel a draft."

"I'm not surprised." She chewed on her lip at the sight of that shoulder wound from which blood was still oozing. Obviously he should be in a hospital for proper treatment. She clamped down on that thought immediately.

Better to be thankful that he could be kept warm and fairly comfortable in the hut until daylight.

"Don't let it throw you, Sue." His tone was understanding. "I've had lots worse things than this. Slap a bandage on and strap it tight."

"Who's the doctor on this case? After watching hospital dramas on television all these years, I don't intend to call in my patient for consultation," she told him haughtily. "Frankly, I was just deciding on my fee."

"The ceiling's the limit. I've never been so glad to see anybody in my life."

She made a final loop with the bandage and secured it before she said briskly, "If you're going to be grateful ... you'll spoil everything. Besides, there was a slight episode in the gold shaft—so now we're even." She let her hand rest gently on his forearm. "Does that bandage feel about right?"

"Fine thanks." There was a flicker of amusement and something else in his glance as he craned his head to look up at her. "What's next on your schedule, nurse?"

"Now I pull you over to the fire and put a blanket around your shoulders. The boots come off and I'll stuff your feet and legs in a down sleeping bag." She was tugging at the camp frame as she spoke. "Then I blow up your pillow and you can rest while I light the lantern and go out to call Cal."

"Call Cal? What the devil are you talking about?"

She smiled. "I forgot that you hadn't seen the inside of Uncle Tim's jeep either. There's a radio under the dashboard."

He frowned and stirred restlessly.

"Take my word for it—everything's going to be all right," she went on hastily. "The explanations will come while you're having something to eat, but now I have to check in with Cal before he calls out the marines."

"Okay, I can wait." He reached over to pat Rock when the dog shifted to lie down by the cot. "Tell Martin we can meet him any time after sunup."

She nodded without speaking as she continued to inflate a rubber pillow and then slipped it carefully under his cheek.

He watched drowsily while she trimmed the wick on the kerosene lamp, lit it, and adjusted the flame before replacing the glass chimney. She watched its steady glow for a minute, then picked up her lantern. "I won't be long," she said softly, glancing back down at him, "sleep if you can."

"I hate to—I might wake up and find I've been dreaming the whole thing."

At that moment, Rock let out a long whistling snore which turned into a lazy groan as he started to scratch his ear. Sue's shoulders heaved with laughter.

"Believe me—you're awake," she assured Nick. "Nobody's dreams could include anything the size of Rock. Soup's on . . . as soon as I get back."

She was gone a mercifully short while.

Either that or he had slept, Nick decided, as he opened his eyes to find her back in the room, busily pouring soup from a vacuum bottle into a plastic drinking cup.

She must have felt his glance because she looked over and smiled. "Ready to take nourishment?"

"I could go for practically anything . . . even those dried candlefish you were telling me about."

"We're fresh out of those. You'll have to make do with split pea soup." Her hands trembled slightly as she came over to kneel beside him. "Sorry to treat you like a baby, but I think you'd better let me feed you. If I prop you up, the movement might start you bleeding again." She concentrated on spooning the hot liquid. "I'll try not to dump this down your neck."

His steady glance was darned disconcerting, she discovered, when she looked up to encounter it. It took an effort to steady her fingers as she broke off bite-sized pieces of pilot bread to drop in the soup for extra nourishment. The silence was heavy, but she refused to babble inanities to fill the void; then he would know for sure what a devastating effect he had upon her.

"There," she said finally in some relief as he finished the last swallow, "that should hold you for a while. Want to rest now?"

He shook his head. "You don't have to coddle me. I'm feeling much better. My only danger was starvation—so don't look so damned skeptical. I still want to know how you managed to get up here."

"You must be getting better ... you're reverting to normal much too fast."

"Uh huh. Back to my obnoxious self."

"At least it's nicer than this afternoon when I was wondering whether I should notify your nearest and dearest before I draped a black swag on the door."

He reached out to grasp her hand. "Stop changing the subject." His voice was definitely stronger. "How did you get that jeep moving?"

"There was nothing miraculous about that. Rock found the missing rotor on the floor when he was retrieving his dog biscuit and don't you dare say anything about 'out of the mouths of babes,'" she said as he chuckled. "I thought the darned thing was gone forever." She pulled away gently to put the cup back on the table and then decided to add a log to the fire. "The rotor, I mean," she added.

"I know what you mean. Stop fluttering around and rest awhile," he commanded. "If you're going to play Good Nurse Sue, you'll have to conserve your strength. Besides, it gives me a crick in the neck to look up at you. Make Rock move over . . . there'll be room for you to sit on the edge of this cot."

"I can manage on the floor."

"Do as I tell you." His voice brooked no interference."

"If you're this bossy when you're sick . . ."

"I'm a holy terror when I'm well. Lennie will confirm that." He pushed back a fold of the blanket impatiently. "Where did you learn how to replace a rotor?"

Her laugh bubbled out. "I told you that being a trade writer provided a fund of information. For a few months, my editors assigned me to *Service Station Management Digest* and I took a course in motor mechanics for self-preservation."

"You don't look like the coverall type."

"I'm not. Before I finished lesson five in the textbook, I was switched to another trade journal, so I dropped the course. The instructor seemed quite relieved," she added sadly.

He started to chuckle and then grimaced. "Ouch! It hurts to laugh."

"Then don't! Besides, it's your turn now—what happened to you?"

"I got damned careless," he growled. "Everything went fine at the beginning. I couldn't see that Florence and her pals had changed any of our stakes or blazes, so I was able to start back across the glacier well before dark. But then I must have been thinking about something else because I made a misstep with my crampon and lost my footing."

"That doesn't sound like being careless...."

"It is when you've left your ice ax looped from your wrist." He sounded thoroughly fed up. "They warn against that on your first climbing lesson."

"So you landed on it when you fell. I was wondering how you got that nasty gash." She put a comforting hand on the back of his wrist. "It must have been a dickens of a trip off the ice."

"It wasn't easy. The cut was in such an awkward place that I couldn't put any pressure on it to stop the bleeding. I finally decided I'd better concentrate on getting off the glacier before I passed out. Fortunately, I knew about this cabin and made for it." He turned his hand and grasped her fingers in his. "Better deduct the price of a pair of crampons and an ice ax from my salary; I shed them as soon as I reached solid ground."

An elusive dimple appeared at the corner of her mouth. "Don't worry—I'll take you to court if you don't make reimbursement. Uncle Tim's lawyer is going to be busy—suing you for absconding with private property ... as well as charging Florence, Leo, and Monica with grand larceny. Or is it grand theft?"

"What are you talking about?"

"Putting the three of them in the hoosegow. Isn't it great?" The firelight reflected her elfin grin. "They might be able to say that Leo sat on the radio by mistake, but they're going to have a dandy time convincing the Coast Guard that I gave them the cruiser for a joy ride."

Nick's grasp on her hand tightened. "Hold it ... go back to the beginning and bring me up to date."

"Hey," she protested, "I plan to use those fingers again."

"Sorry," he loosened his grasp instantly. "*Now* will you put me out of my misery."

"All right—but I'm not much happier with my behavior than you were with yours. Ye gods, I've read about coffee drugged with sleeping potions for years and what do I do? I meekly drain my cup."

"Susan!" his voice thundered, "from the beginning!"

She grinned and capitulated—starting from the time she had left him on the path until the showdown over the coffee mugs with Florence.

He listened attentively until she had finished and then his eyebrows drew together in an ominous line. "I don't understand how you can be so cheerful. Even assuming that Martin is right when he says they haven't docked the cruiser in a Juneau boat basin yet—what's to keep them from beaching it north of town first thing in the morning? They could still get to the Federal Building and try to file that claim before the authorities catch up with them." Shifting restlessly, he went on, "Knowing Florence, she'll be barricaded with attorneys and alibis if she thinks there's any chance of trouble."

Sue shook her head stubbornly. "She won't have a chance to contact her attorney."

"Why not?"

"Because I think I finally did one thing right. It didn't look to me as if she planned to stay around the lodge much longer when she packed away her woodcarving project. And then later when she spoke of the fishing trip, it seemed pretty obvious that she had something longer in mind than a midchannel excursion. The only place I goofed was in thinking they planned to take me along." She sighed and stretched gingerly. "Do you mind if I sit on the floor, after all? That way I can use the cot for a backrest."

"I don't mind if you stand on your head if you'll just...."

"Get on with it," she finished for him as she moved down and leaned against the wooden frame. "Well, the first thing I did was top the first tank of the cruiser with fuel and then filled the other one...."

"So?"

She shook her head. "You won't wait for the punch line. I filled the second one with water. *W**A**T**E**R*—as in *aqua pura, agua, wasser*, etc. etc." She caught at his threatening fist and grinned. "I thought that if Florence was as lily-pure as she claimed, we could get out and back on the fishing jaunt with the first tank. If they planned a longer trip, they'd be well on their way by the time they had to switch over to the second tank and then they wouldn't be going anyplace." She glanced at his intent face. "You're still frowning, Mr. Bones. What's furrowing that intelligent brow?"

"Remind me to turn you over my knee when we get back to civilization," he said absently. "So their engine conks out in midchannel.... What's to keep them from calling for help from one of the trollers or gill-netters passing by?"

"You keep underestimating me," she complained, edging into a more comfortable position. "Not that I don't have a few failings...."

"I warn you, young lady...."

"But not as many as you might think. They aren't going to call for help unless they can find the microphone on the ship-to-shore radio. And the only way they're going to find it is by practically standing on their collective heads in the forward stateroom and pulling out the bottom drawer on the storage locker all the way. After that, they'll have to lie flat on their faces and scrounge at arm's length to reach it. I know," she assumed a becoming modesty, "because I did just that in putting it there."

His eyes were bright with laughter. "May I touch you, Miss Strathern?"

She held up a languid hand. "Only gently, of course," and then spoiled the effect with an infectious giggle. "The thought of Monica scrabbling around on the floor was the one bright spot in my day."

"It sounds as if you did a damned good job."

Her mood sobered. "I hope so. I didn't throw the microphone away because I wasn't sure I was right about that, either. I'd have felt an awful fool if it had been an innocent fishing trip. Now, of course, the Coast Guard should pick them up if they're anchored along the way or come limping in with some borrowed fuel tomorrow morning." She inspected his drawn face thoughtfully. "Let's forget about Florence for the time being. Would you like some of that brandy now? It might help you to sleep."

"No thanks—I won't need it. The heat of the fire has finally penetrated."

"That's good. We have enough wood so that I can keep it going all night."

He scowled. "There's no need for you to be roaming around all night waiting on me. Take that other cot in the corner and get some rest."

Sue stared at him in amazement. Evidently he had indulged in another change of mood and she was left on the outside looking in—again. Why did he persist in erecting barriers higher than the Berlin wall? Couldn't the idiot tell by now that she was completely besotted with him? She could guarantee that there hadn't been any doubts in his mind earlier in the day when they had said goodbye on the boathouse path.

She narrowed her eyes thoughtfully. Of course, he hadn't committed himself to any specific declarations. There was an attraction—certainly. She'd be a fool to deny that; the physical desire was there on both sides. But for Nick . . . possibly it was a passing thing.

She got to her feet abruptly as she remembered Cal's words— "it wouldn't be the first time a gal like you was courted for her tangible assets. . . ."

Nick eyed her warily. "I thought you'd gone into a brown study."

"Nope." Her light tone was a triumph of unconcern, but she had to keep short rein on her self-control. "Brown studies are too much work at this time of night." Damn the man, she thought bitterly. Wasn't there anything he missed? It was like being thrown against a mind reader—and the way her mind was acting, she was hopelessly vulnerable.

Her glance lit on Rock, who had decided to wake up and find another pastime. "Stop shredding that log," she scolded. "We'll probably need it before morning."

The brown crook of a tail wagged lazily as he paused in his work and looked up hopefully. There was always the chance she might offer something better—like food.

"Come on, tiger." She prodded him with a gentle toe. "You'd better go out for a few minutes."

He bounded up at that magic word and followed her to the door.

"I'll keep an eye on him," she said carefully over her shoulder. "He's inclined to head for the Arctic Circle unless he's told otherwise." She waited for a comment from the quiet figure by the fire and when it wasn't forthcoming, shut the cabin door firmly behind her.

As soon as it had closed, Nick raised his head to stare at the door, a hard-to-read expression on his face. His right hand doubled into a fist and he pounded it gently on the frame of the bed. "Damn!" he finally said in frustration and let his head flop down again.

By the time Sue had corralled Rock back into the room, she had blinked away the suspicious moisture in her eyes and was ready to demonstrate her ability to fend for herself, the masculine sex notwithstanding.

She hauled the other camp frame into use and placed it a discreet ten feet away from Nick's. Her air mattress was inflated and her sleeping bag unrolled neatly on top of it. Then, wordlessly, she extinguished the kerosene lamp to let the firelight provide the only illumination.

Keeping well away from Nick's quiet figure, she moved over and added another log to the blaze. As she stooped down to dispose of Rock's wood chips, she heard Nick move restlessly and caught the tail end of his irritated look.

"Why not hang a bell around my neck if you intend to treat me like a leper," he said grimly as she straightened. "The atmosphere's so thick in here you could cut it with a knife."

"I'm merely following your suggestion." She dusted her hands elaborately. "You told me to go to bed. . . . I'm going to bed. What could be simpler than that?"

"You don't have to act as if I'd sent you to the stake."

"I'm not acting like anything of the sort," she flared. "Forgive me if I miss some of my cues, but I don't know you well enough to be clairvoyant." She shoved her hands deep in her jacket pockets. "Even Florence has the advantage of me there . . . she was letting slip all sorts of goodies about your past life."

"I'll bet she was." He kicked the sleeping bag away from his feet irritably. "If I'd known everybody was so interested, I could have published my memoirs."

"I am not in the least interested in your past

life," she said, lying in her teeth. "At the moment, I'm merely concerned with seeing you get to Cal's plane for pickup in the morning. After that, I'm sure you can manage to take care of yourself. I know darned well that I can!" The toe of her boot pushed their remaining woodpile into line with a violence that made Rock start nervously six feet away.

"God . . . give me strength," Nick grated out. "Now listen to me, Sue Strathern. After tomorrow, I'll explain the whole ball of wax with ruffles and flourishes. In the meantime . . . I told you . . . you'll have to trust me."

"I *do* trust you. I just don't see why the dickens you have to suddenly turn into a puritan father and make me feel like a . . ." her voice trailed off.

"A what?"

"You know darned well what I mean."

He compressed his lips. "How old are you, Sue?"

"Twenty-four. What has that to do with anything?"

"At twenty-four, I shouldn't have to explain things to you." The lines of weariness were etched deeply around his eyes. "Do you realize this is the third night we've spent alone together? You can scrub the first night; it didn't mean a thing. The night after the mine episode wasn't so easy . . . I told you about that." His face was devoid of expression. "And tonight . . .

well, the fact that I've wrecked my shoulder doesn't mean that I'm completely dead in all other parts." He let the words sink in. "You're damned attractive, Miss Strathern . . . even in a pair of wrinkled slacks and a shapeless jacket."

Sue heard Rock scratching at the floor and wished he could dig a hole big enough for her to disappear into.

"Shall I go on?" Nick's voice was even. "Or do I make myself clear?"

"Very clear." The lilt was back in her words. "My uncle could tell you I'm a slow learner . . . I apologize. My only excuse is that I haven't had much experience along this line."

His lips twitched only once—then he said dryly, "I think that's just as well." The thongs creaked beneath him as he settled back. "What time do we leave in the morning?"

"Sunrise comes at five-eleven. I told Cal we'd be at the pickup spot on the river at six-fifteen. If we're not there, he'll beach the plane and start hiking this way."

"We'll be there."

"I hope so."

"Why so pessimistic all of a sudden?"

"Well, I was in a hurry when I was tossing in provisions for breakfast. . . ."

"And?"

Her soft lips twitched in glee. "The only thing I remembered was a package of dehydrated eggs."

He groaned. "In that case, I'll buy you breakfast in Juneau. But now...."

"I know—go to bed." It was hard to maintain a semblance of poise when she felt her resistance ebb. "Good night, Nick. Call me if you want anything...." The words trailed off under his frankly amused look. "If your bandage needs changing," she finished feebly.

"I will. Good night, Sue... and thanks."

From outside, there came a chilling howl that arrested her footsteps. Nick heard it too.

"A wolf," he confirmed, as the dismal sound floated away. "Do you keep him around to provide sound effects for the eastern visitors, or is he for my benefit?"

"What on earth do you mean?"

"My namesake... that totem you were telling about called Tired Wolf. Damned if the label doesn't fit tonight. You were right, after all."

She issued instructions to the shaggy dog who was looking on. "If Mr. Dunbar moves off that cot tonight—bite him. And if you get bored later on—bite him then too. It'll serve him right."

Long ago, Shakespeare wrote about the "slow passage of time." He probably had something else on his mind in the sixteenth century, Sue decided, but spending a night in a sleeping bag brought his words agonizingly to mind in the twentieth.

The first time she looked at her watch, it was five minutes after eleven. The second time it was eleven-thirty. After that it narrowed to ten-minute intervals for what seemed to be an eternity. Each passing minute strengthened the rigidity of those leather thongs and by two o'clock in the morning, Sue would have sworn she was lying on a block of concrete; every aching bone in her body confirmed it.

After such exquisite suffering, it was a special indignity that she fell soundly asleep around three-thirty and wasn't conscious of another thing until she heard Nick's voice saying "C'mon lady—it's five-fifteen. Are you going to sleep all day?"

She lay motionless, her eyes tightly closed, feeling like a leftover death hadn't bothered to warm up.

"If ever there was provocation for justifiable homicide," she managed finally between clenched teeth, "this is it." She focused on his upright form with difficulty. "Rock could rend you limb from limb and I could scatter your bones for the wolves. No one would ever know."

"You could try," he admitted judicially. "However, I've just fed your hound an entire box of crackers and he's been washing my hands for the past five minutes as a result—so it might be difficult to get your orders across. Are you going to get vertical soon or do you need further pursuasion?"

With an effort, she opened her eyes all the way and saw that his hair was damp from recent combing and that he'd managed to wash his face. Even with an overnight growth of beard, there was a spruceness about him.

"I'll get there any minute now," she promised. "What are you doing up?"

"I thought one of us should be."

"That's not what I mean. How do you feel?"

"Not bad . . . all things considered. How about you?"

"Don't ask." She pushed out of the sleeping bag with an effort and fumbled on the floor for her boots. "You'd better stay quiet or you'll start the bleeding again."

"I'll be careful. Would you like a cup of coffee?"

She nodded and started to pull on her boots only to encounter a cold nose and a moist tongue. "Rock—stop it," she commanded, pushing his wriggling form to one side. "I need more refurbishing than you can manage, thanks."

"Here—have a cup of coffee and stop struggling." Nick pushed a plastic cup into her hand and sat down gingerly beside her. "I hope you didn't want cream or sugar."

She managed a smile. "I didn't expect to get them. Don't forget, I packed the basket." She sipped the steaming liquid carefully. "Has your shoulder really stopped bleeding?"

"I think so." He watched her shove back a strand of hair from her face. "Stop fussing ... you look fine."

"Mr. Dunbar ... sir ... you are a charming liar—but thanks all the same. Ummm, this coffee helps."

He nodded absently. "I'm leery about doing much bending to pack properly so let's just toss the essential stuff in the back of the jeep."

"Of course." She drained the coffee and stood up. "Do me a favor and stay right there while I get it ready." She watched a look of indecision pass over his drawn features. "Look ... Nick, be sensible," she urged. "You have to be on your feet when we get to Juneau and before that we have a rugged jeep ride and a plane trip. This stuff isn't heavy; I'll throw some of it in the jeep and leave the rest. Joe can get it later." She brushed his shoulder lightly. "Will you forget that you're a gentleman just this once and let me do the work?"

"All right . . . thanks." He shifted to a straight chair by the table. "I'll act as straw boss."

"You can also keep Rock out of the way. He's been known to unload the jeep faster than I can put things in."

Her first trip to the jeep revealed the weather had turned crisp and clear. She took a deep breath of the Taku wind off the glacier's icy slopes and found it had the same effect as a brisk morning shower. Overhead, the sunrise diffused its colors across the sky, not the muted pinks of the warmer latitudes but ribbons of pale yellow threading through gray clouds.

When the jeep was finally loaded, she spread a sturdy tarp over the top of the provisions so that Rock could perch on it. "He's a little big for a lap dog," she told Nick solemnly as they went out of the hut, "although he pictures himself that way."

He snorted and hoisted himself into the jeep. "Some lap dog! It would be like fondling a walrus. Come on, boy," he whistled for the cavorting terrier. "Drop that piece of firewood first! Oh for Lord's sake—not there!"

Sue stopped him as he was about to crawl out and retrieve it from the track. "I'll get it. Rocko—get in that car and behave yourself."

She was only in the cabin for a minute before she returned to the driver's seat. "You did a nice job taking care of the fire," she said, reaching for the ignition switch.

"Part of a caretaker's duties," he assured her solemnly.

"Ummm." As she drove off, she gave him a worried look. "Hang on, will you? I'll take it as easy as I can, but this road is rough."

He nodded. "Where do we meet Martin?"

"There's a bend in the river right after it

flows out of the lake. It's a natural little inlet where the water is calm. The bank has a fairly steep drop-off so he can bring the floats right alongside."

The jeep lurched into a deep rut and his jaw tightened, but he made no comment.

"I'm sorry," Sue said. "Your shoulder must be giving you fits."

"Just keep going and forget it. I'm damned glad to be riding. Even the hope of walking seemed pretty remote yesterday." He searched for a cigarette and lit it. "Don't forget to have somebody collect those crampons and that ice ax."

"I'll tell Joe to look for them when he goes to the cabin." She glanced sideways at him. "I take it that you won't be around to recuperate at the lodge?"

" 'Fraid not." He wedged his head and arm against the side of the jeep to keep the jolting to a minimum. "I have some things to do first." His tone was as casual as hers. "I'll be back though."

She managed a creditable smile. "Don't forget to apply for the off-season rates when you come."

He reached out and ran his finger caressingly along the back of her hand. "You could be checking on yearly rates in the meantime. Hey, look out! You'll have us off the road."

"I don't know why I didn't leave you lying helpless on the floor."

"I can't imagine myself. Is it much further?"

She shook her head. "The track forks down here a little further. How's the time?"

He glanced at his watch. "We're in good shape and we don't have to worry about weather conditions, so Martin should be there. I wonder what Florence told that flying service I hired when she switched pickup times?"

"Something convincing, no doubt. She was good at things like that. We'd better ask Cal to radio them and cancel completely."

"Lord yes." He rubbed his forehead wearily. "I should have thought of that."

"You're entitled to function at half-speed for a day or two," she assured him. "Here's our turnoff. Hang on tight—this part is the worst yet."

Fortunately there was only a short distance to cover down the steep hillside until they came out of the trees onto the river bank.

"There's the inlet," Sue said. "I'll run the jeep as close as I dare."

Behind them, Rock whined in excitement, sensing the end of their ride.

"Stay put," she commanded him tersely. "There isn't time for you to go gallivanting."

She cut the engine on a rocky ledge where the river lapped a bare foot beneath. Out in midstream, the physical makeup of the river changed completely with the muddy silt from the glacier kept apart from the creek water and hillside runoff. But Sue was disregarding color of the water when she hunched down in the jeep and carefully surveyed the length of that slow-moving surface.

"It looks clear," she said finally in relief. "Cal will do some looking of his own, though, before he lands."

"Icebergs?"

She nodded. "One reason that bush pilots are darned careful."

"I suppose the ones who weren't died long ago. Listen . . ." he rubbed out his cigarette and held up a warning hand. "I think I hear him."

A pleased smile flickered over her face. "Smack on time—he's wonderful!"

They watched the small plane buzz over the treetops like a busy mosquito and then follow the course of the river.

"I think I can manage something more tangible than gratitude for him," Nick said quietly.

"What do you mean?" And then before he offered an evasive answer, she gave a rueful half-shake of her head. "Never mind—I won't ask any more questions."

He merely reached across and caught her fingers in a quick, hard squeeze. "Good girl. Here he comes for the landing."

She hopped out of the jeep. "I want you to stay where you are until he's alongside."

"Don't worry . . . Rock and I'll both stay put."

Sue was waiting on the bank when Cal taxied the small Cessna into the quiet water. He maneuvered alongside and tossed her a line through the opened cabin door before cutting the engine.

"Hang on, Susie." He made fast his end of the line and then was out of the plane and up onto the bank beside her. "Top of the morning to you, honey. How's the invalid?" he asked, jerking his head toward the jeep. "And how are you?"

"Both fine—now that you're here." She reached up and patted his cheek happily. "Oh Cal, I'm glad to see you!"

"Cut it out, woman!" He removed her hand carefully. "Judging from the scowl that just appeared on your passenger's face, I'd say his condition was deteriorating. Any more of that and he'll have a stroke. I'll take my thanks at a later date." He moved over to the jeep and bent down to assist Nick. "Good morning, Mr. Dunbar. Sorry you've had such a bad time."

"Thanks." The other stepped cautiously out of the jeep. "You can skip that Mr. Dunbar business . . . the name's Nick."

"All right, Nick. Let's get you over to the plane."

"Good god, man . . ." Nick shook off the helping hand at his elbow. "I don't know what Sue told you, but I don't have to be treated like perishable cargo."

There came an anguished howl from the rear of the jeep.

"Stop it, Rock!" Sue commanded. "And you—Nick," she put her hands on her waist truculently, "do as Cal tells you and stop being so darned stubborn. This is no time to go all stiff-necked and masculine. Please . . ."

There was an astounded silence from both men.

Finally Nick's face creased in a sheepish grin. "All right, Sue. Drop your guns—I surrender." He looked at Cal. "How do you want to manage this?"

It would have taken an expert to discern any bleakness in Cal's expression and certainly no fault could be found with his manner. "See if you can edge across the float," he instructed, "and ease yourself up into the place beside mine. Sue will have to hang onto that line while I get the pooch on board. I'll be lucky if both of us don't land in the briny before that's accomplished."

"Okay—give me a couple of minutes until I can get in," Nick said, "then I can help steer Rock into the cabin."

At any other time, the sight of Cal clasping eighty pounds of excited Airedale in his arms would have had Sue doubled over with laughter. As it was, she was holding her breath as Cal threaded his way across the bobbing float until Nick could grasp Rock's thick collar with his good hand and maneuver him into the back of the cabin.

Cal sighed loudly when the dog was safely inside. "Next time I'll tell Tim to buy a chihuahua. What a lump that beast is!"

"Be thankful he's not a Saint Bernard." Sue was flip in relief after the successful tranfer.

"And you, woman ... better be careful or I'll leave you on the bank," Cal threatened.

"You couldn't do that," she told him. "Rock wouldn't let me be left behind."

"I don't suppose Nick would either ... if it came to that." Cal was intent on fastening his seat belt. "Is that right, Dunbar?"

"Got it in one." The other was emphatic.

"That's what I thought. So—I'm outnumbered, Susie." Cal shot her a mocking grin. "Better come aboard now. Let's get out of here." He waited for her to crawl in behind him and pulled the door shut behind her. "Fasten your seat belts. Nick?"

Dunbar nodded.

"Sue?" There was no answer and Cal peered over his shoulder. "What's the trouble back there?"

"No trouble really. My seat belt's fastened, but Cal ..." her voice trailed off.

"What's the matter?"

"How do you put a seat belt on an Airedale? Oh ... never mind," she went on finally when she could make herself heard over their laughter. "He's on my lap and I'll keep him there."

Cal reached for the mag switch. "In that case, I'll only charge him half-fare. We'll probably have to scrape you off the seat with a pancake turner when we get to Juneau." He set the throttles. "Let's go."

The trip back was uneventful. Nick's shoulder was evidently paining him more than he would admit as he sat white-faced and weary with his head resting against the side of the plane. Once they had taken off, he asked Cal to contact his office and get word to Lennie Brock to meet them at the Northland pier with a waiting taxi. "She'll be expecting a call," he said simply.

Cal nodded. "Lennie gave me the word. You rank with the chosen ones as far as she's concerned." He managed a sideways grin. "Otherwise you wouldn't be getting this service."

"I suspected it was out of the ordinary. How come Lennie's taking up the defense for me?"

"Beats me—you'd better ask her. Since she furnished a good part of my operating capital, I didn't quibble," Cal said frankly. "But even Lennie couldn't have changed my mind on some other things if I hadn't seen for myself. One of the first things a pilot has to know is which way the wind is blowing. You're damn lucky."

"I'm well aware of that."

Sue leaned forward as far as she could over Rock's solid form. "I can only hear bits and snatches," she complained.

Nick half-turned in his seat. "You're not missing a thing," he assured her.

"There's nothing new on Florence?"

Cal shook his head. "Not when I took off and I checked to be sure. The officer in charge of the Coast Guard ship is a friend of mine." The sardonic grin flashed again. "He didn't see how they could possibly locate them and bring them back to town before nine this morning."

"Thanks, Cal," Nick said. "I appreciate that, but he doesn't have to allow so much time. My business shouldn't take more than about five minutes and the land office opens at eight sharp. If Lennie brings the papers I left with her, I plan to be on the doorstep of the Federal Building when they unlock the doors."

"And I'm going to be there with you," Sue informed him. "I want to be sure you get there first even if I have to tackle Florence in the hallway."

"Make that three of us," Cal said. "You might need some more muscles."

"Good idea," Sue nodded. "You can help with Leo if you have to."

"Damn! I was planning a running block on Monica."

"Wouldn't you know..." Sue solemnly addressed the Airedale draped across her lap. "Sex is on a man's mind even at a time like this."

Nick roused himself to give her a look which made her cheeks flame. "I was wondering," he said whimsically, "when you'd get around to noticing it."

Chapter Ten

The promise of a clear autumn day had deteriorated into the certainty of a rainy morning when they arrived at Cal's pier in Juneau.

Sue assessed her wrinkled outfit and Nick's bristly chin. "The way we're dressed, we'll probably be arrested for vagrancy by the first policeman." She was clutching Rock's collar to keep him from plunging around the dock until Cal fashioned a makeshift leash.

"It's a good thing we're not out to impress anybody," Nick granted.

"Don't worry, I'll vouch for you," Cal told him blandly. He finished knotting the rope and handed the end of it to Sue. "That should keep the pooch where you want him."

"Thanks, Cal." She gave Nick an anxious glance. "Don't forget, you're checking in at the hospital as soon as you finish at the land office."

They were walking slowly up the ramp to the street.

"We'll see," he said noncommittally.

"Look! There's our reception committee...." Cal pointed to a waiting cab at the curbside with Lennie standing by the open door. "She promised to have things under control."

"And I have," the older woman said, overhearing his words. "I wouldn't have missed this for a mess of greens. Get in the car this minute, Nicholas, before you measure your length on the sidewalk."

"I'm all right, Lennie." He hung onto the rear door. "Did you bring the envelope?"

"Certainly. It's right in my bag, young man." Her tone was tart, but she gave him a brief hug before saying, "We'll put you in the car by force if we have to."

"Hold it," Nick said, capitulating. "I'm practically in." He slid onto the back seat carefully.

"I'll sit up in front," Cal said. "Sue ... you and Lennie get in beside him."

"Mrs. Brock says you folks all want to go to the Federal Building," the driver said as they crowded in.

"That's right," Nick told him. He looked over at Lennie as the car moved off. "Is there apt to be any trouble?"

"Nary a bit. That option of yours should go through in record time. There's been no word from the Coast Guard yet; Cal can call their base later on. Incidentally, the land office will be open when we get to the Federal Building. There's nothing in the statutes that says it has to open at eight and the man in charge decided they'd start business a little early this morning. He'll be ready to receive your option as soon as you can deliver it."

Relief washed over Nick's drawn features. "My lord, Lennie—is there anything you can't accomplish in this town?"

"It didn't take much persuasion, boy. Half the population of Juneau's in on this by now, and we've been waiting a long time for Florence to get what she deserves." She nodded sagely. "When she buys her way out of this mess, it wouldn't surprise me if she went back to the lower forty-eight and stayed there." She turned to Sue. "When you're putting in a bill for the use of that cruiser and the other things—I'd make it sizable."

"Don't worry. I certainly intend to."

"And plan to stay with me while you're in town," Lennie added. "I'd enjoy your company and you can bring your dog along." She reached down to pat a quivering Rock whose nose was glued rapturously to the window.

"Thank you—we accept with pleasure," Sue said gratefully. "I'd better go in by your back door until I look more presentable."

"Pshaw, girl!" The other wrinkled her nose disdainfully. "You should know by now that folks in Alaska don't set store by outside trappings."

The cab slowed to a stop in front of a tall office building.

"Guess we've arrived," Lennie said. She reached into her bag and hauled out a thick manila envelope, which she gave to Nick. "I won't try to stop you from delivering this in person but let Cal go along just in case. . . ."

Nick was beyond arguing. "Okay, Lennie. Let's go, Cal."

Lennie and Sue watched the two men cross the wide sidewalk and disappear into the lobby, which was just beginning to come alive with workers.

"Nick walks like he can hardly manage another step," Lennie said in a worried tone.

"He lost a lot of blood." Sue found her hands were clutched tightly on Rock's leash and she relaxed to flex her fingers. "It must be sheer will power that's keeping him going by now—I've been afraid he'd collapse all morning."

"Don't worry," Lennie patted her arm. "The hospital is the next stop. My doctor promised to stand by there in the emergency room." She smiled. "He's a hardheaded type like I am; Nick won't get out of there until he's fit again." She leaned closer. "Just between the two of us, I even held off on confirming his plane reservation."

Here came the news with a vengeance, Sue thought. She tried to make her voice matter-of-fact as she asked, "Where's he off to this time?"

"New York. His bosses want him to report in person." Lennie's lips thinned to a straight line. "They can just wait a few days until he's fit to be traipsing around the country again."

Sue smoothed the shaggy hair on Rock's neck for something to do. If New York was next on Nick's schedule, it could be weeks before he returned to Alaska. She cleared her throat and said, "Excitement must be second nature to Nick. I don't think anything or anybody could hold him back. When do you think we'll see him again?"

Lennie's eyes gleamed. "I gathered you'd have the inside track on that news. Nick just told me to make a round-trip reservation for New York." She paused suggestively. "He also said that if things looked as if they were going to drag on too long back there—they could get along without him. My goodness . . ." her words choked off as she was hugged enthusiastically by the young woman beside her. When she could talk again, she said "And I thought you were clever, Sue. You've had the man wrapped up and delivered all this time. I even told Cal to stand back—he's a nice boy, but there's lots of time for him to get married. Now Nick though . . ." her expression softened, "Nick is different. You were meant to be together."

Sue was still cherishing those words on a pleasant afternoon three weeks later.

Fortunately, she decided, other circumstances had changed considerably in the interval. The disreputable outfit she had been wearing, for example, was now replaced by a *soignée* Irish designer suit of off-white wool. Soft brown leather trimmed the collar and jacket pockets while the skirt flared into graceful pleats. Her rough hiking boots had been exchanged for alligator pumps whose heels were much too elegant for standing on the slippery stern decking of Captain Fergus' mail boat. This became evident as she grabbed frantically for the railing when the vessel hit a patch of rough water.

"Hey—take it easy, beautiful," Nick laughed as he moved quickly to steady her. "I don't want to lose you overboard now—not after it took all this time for us to get together." He put a protective arm around her waist and urged her toward the rough wooden seat topping a storage locker. "Sit down there."

"All right, thanks. Did you finish stowing your luggage in the wheelhouse?" It was hard for Sue to subdue the lilt in her voice when asking a prosaic question, harder still to believe that the tanned, fit man sitting beside her was real at all.

"All neatly taken care of. Incidentally, that special box is for Rocko. I decided he needed something for chewing other than Wickitak's entire winter supply of firewood."

"Good heavens—you must have brought enough toys for a month. He won't want to stir away from that box."

"That was the general idea," he said calmly, ignoring her quick glance.

"He'll be delighted anyway," she assured him. "I had him trimmed during his stay at Lennie's and he's so fashionable-looking these days that he spends most of his time admiring his whiskers in the mirror."

"No more shaggy dog?"

"The exterior isn't so rough, but otherwise he's just the same."

He smiled. "Good. I like him that way. By the way, the captain says we're to help ourselves to coffee when we feel like it. He also said to tell you that he's not being as sociable as usual because he thought we'd like to have some time alone."

"He's positively psychic." Sue smiled over at Nick's relaxed form. "You know, I still can't believe this; I've been pinching myself ever since we got aboard the boat. If that plane of yours had been fifteen minutes later, I would have exploded into little pieces from the excitement."

"I know—but we were an hour late leaving Chicago, so what could you expect? At this time of year, it's lucky I made connections at all." He leaned back and took a deep breath. "You must have special influence with the weatherman up here. This is a real Indian summer day."

"Probably it was Lennie's doing. I was too

unstrung to concentrate on anything practical although she was pretty excited herself when you finally appeared."

"You mean when we ran her down at the chapel?"

Sue nodded. "She was thrilled to see you looking so well."

"You both fussed too much about an overnight stay in the hospital."

"There was the small matter of a transfusion and a few other things before you went east."

"At least, it's all over now," he said, shrugging it off. "Except when I need an excuse for not moving on this vacation."

"You won't have to do a thing. Joe and Marie are back on the job and they're nursing the motor generator these nights." She tilted her head and eyed him quizzically. "Besides, you look much too elegant in that dark gray suit to do any manual labor. My mother warned me about city slickers like you."

"Is that all she warned you about?"

"No ... there was a session on the birds and the bees too." The gentle breeze felt comforting on her hot cheeks. "So you needn't have implied that I was a trifle dimwitted on that last flight with Cal. Some of those thoughts had occurred to me even before your kind suggestion, sir."

"Some of those thoughts have occurred to me

in the three weeks I've been gone too," he admitted calmly.

"Then might I suggest you stay put for a while," she said. "Otherwise, I'll buy you a book of commuter tickets for the Juneau-New York run and I'll take up a new hobby."

"A new hobby sounds good. I need to concentrate on something else for the next few weeks." He reached over and flicked a finger down her cheek. "Any suggestions?"

She felt a shiver go down her spine. "Look out, mister! I think you're actually flirting with me. And we've got witnesses!" She pointed upward.

Overhead, two gulls were swooping down on the staff at the mail boat's stern, where the American flag was fluttering easily in the breeze. Another plump white gull banked gracefully by the railing, uttered its mournful cry, and then glided on ahead as a volunteer pilot.

Nick chuckled. "You're right . . . I'd better be careful." He looked over his shoulder toward the bow. "Fergus has eyes in the back of his head too." He settled back on the bench. "After three weeks, there's nothing like a secluded meeting place."

"Well, there certainly wasn't one in Juneau. Lennie and Cal were so nice, though, that we couldn't be annoyed." She frowned suddenly. "How did it happen that Cal changed his mind about you so drastically? Next thing you know, he'll be sponsoring you for the Chamber of Commerce."

His features sobered. "Cal's working hard at being a good sport, but it doesn't come easy."

"He'll bounce back," she said thoughtfully. "Lennie was telling about an attractive blonde secretary who was transferred to Anchorage six months ago when Northland opened its office up there. Now that charter business has improved down here in the southeast, Cal hopes to bring her back. You had something to do with that, didn't you?"

"Not the blonde." Amusement was back in the level gray eyes. "My company did retain Northland for additional transportation to the site."

"That same company which writes your paycheck and sends you off to Mozambique when you're not pulling the wool over innocent women's eyes?"

"No such thing. Your eyes are such a pretty blue that I wouldn't stoop to such chicanery."

"Not much you wouldn't. Do all cadastral engineers act like you? No—don't answer that," she added hastily, "I'd rather not know."

"Well, don't let it worry you," he said soothingly. "They pay me to do other things."

"But how did you get involved with this? That land of Uncle Tim's wasn't much good for anything. I know—because I've been rack-ing my brain ever since you left. Finally, I thought there'd been some new mineral discovery on it. That came after a lengthy process of elimination. I knew oil was out," she was ticking off on her fingers. "The north slope has the whammy on that and their proposed pipeline is hundreds of miles away." A second finger went down. "There's timber on it, but there's nothing new about that. And Uncle Tim always said that he didn't want it logged-off for pulp. So that left mining. . . ." This time, Nick turned the third finger down and somehow forgot to release it in the process. Her voice faltered and then steadied as she went on determinedly. "I haunted all the experts; they told me they're mining barite and prospecting for copper, nickel, and iron around here. But that's not the answer, is it?"

He shook his head. "Sorry Sherlock ... you just didn't go far enough."

"Well then—*you* tell me."

"Fair enough. You've been very patient. Now listen—with all the rainfall and lakes in the mountains around here, this part of the state is a natural for power sites. When you have power sites, industry follows. Look, my dear," he pushed back a silky strand of hair from her brow and leaned closer. "There's a potential here of a million year-around horsepower. At the moment, they've only developed sixty-five thousand of it. Do you wonder that my company's excited?" He went on, "The construction of the power plant was all signed, sealed, and ready to be delivered. The next thing we had to arrange was the locating of a pipeline for coal delivery to it from the Yukon River country."

"Coal ... in a pipeline?" Her voice rose in amazement.

He nodded. "That's right ... coal in a pipeline. It's called slurry form. By going across your uncle's land, we saved a devil of a lot of mileage and expense. His option on the property was about to expire. It was perfectly fine with him that my company file a new option so long as he could utilize the land for the lodge as he always has."

"How did Florence come into this?"

"Florence wanted the property solely for a club to hold over our heads. She knew about the power plant and she knew we needed the pipeline. We could have purchased pipeline rights from her—at an exorbitant price. The damnable part was—as soon as I had gotten Tim's agreement not to renew his option, Florence had as good a chance for the land as anybody else. It was strictly first come, first served."

"But you weren't suspicious of her when you first arrived?"

"Not a bit," he admitted. "They seemed a queer trio, but it wasn't until someone searched my things that I tumbled to what might be going on. Lennie's story about her background confirmed it."

"I wonder how she found out about your part in it originally?"

"That wasn't hard. While we didn't publicize the power plant construction, it's difficult to keep a project of that size completely under wraps." He grinned down at her. "There were quite a few of your . . . 'cadavers' . . . working on the site originally. By the time we realized we needed your uncle's property for the pipeline, he'd taken off for his African trip. Since I was familiar with the project, the New York office decided I should go to Mozambique and discuss it with him."

"No wonder you looked so tanned and fit when you got back here," she said accusingly. "Why in the world didn't you say you'd been talking to Uncle Tim?"

"Because I was sworn to secrecy. Lennie wouldn't have known about that trip if an airline reservations clerk hadn't left word about a flight confirmation."

Sue still looked suspicious. "Was accepting a caretaker's job part of your original plan?"

The corners of his mouth twitched as he shook his head. "That job was strictly manna from heaven. Captain Fergus thought I was merely another of Tim's clients and you seemed determined to employ me as soon as I got off the boat. I decided taking the job was the simplest way to keep an eye on things for a few days. At least, until I could file my option in Juneau." He lit a cigarette and dropped his lighter back in his pocket. "There hasn't been a chance to ask what happened to Florence and her pals. Did you finally have her thrown in the local pokey?"

"No—there wasn't any point in putting the taxpayers to additional expense. By the time the Coast Guard put a line on the cruiser and towed them in—you were flat on your back in the hospital and the land option was safely filed."

"Where did they find the cruiser?"

"Leo had finally managed to anchor in one of the inlets about halfway from the lodge. I guess it was pretty uncomfortable when they were adrift."

"How did you find out about all this?"

"Uncle Tim's lawyer met them on the pier." Her laughter bubbled out. "Apparently they were the saddest trio he had ever seen when they finally set foot on solid ground. They'd been seasick for hours—ever since the cruiser lost power. Leo had every kind of medicine in his luggage except pills for motion sickness. When our lawyer told Florence what had happened, she agreed to pay for all damages to the cruiser and replace the radio on condition that I forget about filing criminal charges. It seemed like a fair bargain and Uncle Tim can decide how much to charge her when he returns." She watched him inhale thoughtfully and flick some ashes in a pail of sand before she went on, "According to Lennie, Monica left town before the other two. She must have decided that there wasn't a paycheck big enough to cover Leo's symptoms and that night on the drifting cruiser."

"I wonder how she ever connected with them in the first place?"

"Maybe she made a specialty of silent but susceptible caretakers in the past."

He cocked a warning eyebrow. "Keep it up, madam. You're asking for it."

She gave him a brazen look. "On the other hand, you can scratch that word susceptible. I should know."

"You don't know anything yet, lady." He flicked his cigarette overboard and firmly captured her hand. "But you might find out in the next week or so."

"Is that a threat or a promise?"

"Definitely a promise." He cupped her face between his hands then and said, "Maybe we could set up some preliminary groundwork," before he bent forward and kissed her gently.

Somewhere along the way, the nature of that kiss changed into something possessive, demanding, and thoroughly breathtaking.

Sue finally pulled away to breathe and rest

her cheek on his broad chest. "Oh lord," she murmured unsteadily, trying to decide if it was her heartbeat causing the thundering in her ears or if it could be Nick's. "If that's a preliminary, I'll never survive the main event. I didn't know I could feel like this."

It was as if she were divided into two parts, one part of her managing to conduct a conversation while the other was still reliving that kiss. Nick hadn't needed to commit himself in words. A man couldn't respond like that unless he was as much in love and completely vulnerable as she was.

Thank heavens they had kept a firm grip on conventions when they were alone before. With a man like Nick around, it was safer that way. But not, she decided, half as much fun. Anyway, she was tired of being sensible.

Nick had difficulty steadying his own voice. "I think we'd better discuss my qualifications for employment," he said finally.

"Certainly ... the job's still open for an assistant caretaker," she told him, wondering how she could sound so calm.

He let her push back just slightly before his clasp tightened again. "I might consider it. How about the wages these days?"

"Nothing but the very best."

"Any fringe benefits? A man has to consider things like that." His voice was solemn.

She matched his tone. "I realize that.

Wickitak provides excellent working conditions. You can have every Sunday off and when the cohos are running ... no one expects you to report before noon."

"I'd want to be sure of the accommodations."

"Well, there isn't any television, but there are other things to compensate. Since the season's over, you could occupy the suite at the end of the hall. There's a fireplace, private bath, and complete privacy when you want it."

"Breakfast in bed?"

She swallowed hard. "You drive a hard bargain, but it's possible." Her lashes went down demurely. "We could discuss it later ... later tonight."

He pursed his lips and considered. "I'll promise to think about it."

"There's just one thing. Uncle Tim doesn't approve of transient help. This is a job for a married man."

"No problem there." One finger was gently tracing the soft line of her cheek. "I can qualify on that ever since this afternoon. There's a special license in my pocket to prove it. This *is* a permanent job, I hope?" He dropped a fleeting kiss in the faint hollow of her throat and his caressing hands moved purposefully down from her shoulders.

"Mmmm." Her bones were melting again. "Beyond a doubt. Do you think we could review your qualifications, Mr. Dunbar?"

Then there was no more repartee and no more discussion. Nick pulled her to him roughly as if he couldn't hold off any longer. She wondered if her ribs would crack ... and then forgot to think as his lips parted hers.

It was a lifetime later before he raised his head. "I forgot to mention anything about love, Mrs. Dunbar, but we can discuss that when the moon comes up. Now—do I get the job?"

"Nick ... my darling idiot!" Her adoring glance mirrored all that was in her heart as she reached over to pull his head back down. "Just try and get away!"